Dear Reader,

In your hands is one of my favorite reads of the year! The Dade family—or the "dead family"—was an idea I had for many years. A dear friend of mine inspired it by sharing stories about the little ghosts in his house, which happens to be near a cemetery. The ghosts were very mischievous, he said, and weren't mean-spirited at all. I kept this idea for a long time and then began to build a family around it. What if half the family were dead, but it made no difference at all? Mom still made breakfast, brothers were still annoying . . .

For years I turned this story over in my head, but I had taken it as far as it could go. So we started looking for a writer who would bring this story to life, who (ahem) would breathe new life into the dead. Kitty Curran not only brought the Dades to life, she built an entire world around it. It's the novel in my head perfected, with so much humor and heart and love and hilarity that I cried the first time I read it.

The book touches on those themes that I felt but could not articulate. What happens to people we love when they die? What happens to us? And what if—they could just come back? Wouldn't that be marvelous?

Kitty tells this story complete with mystery, intrigue, middle school drama, and family love. I love this book. I hope you do, too.

xoxo

Melissa de la Cruz

 MELISSA de la CRUZ STUDIO

Grave Mistakes

A DADE FAMILY NOVEL

Grave Mistakes

A DADE FAMILY NOVEL

By KITTY CURRAN

 MELISSA de la CRUZ STUDIO

DISNEP • HYPERION
Los Angeles   New York

Copyright © 2023 Disney Enterprises, Inc.

All rights reserved. Published by Disney • Hyperion, an imprint of Buena Vista Books, Inc.
No part of this book may be reproduced or transmitted in any form or by any means,
electronic or mechanical, including photocopying, recording, or by any information storage
or retrieval system, without written permission from the publisher. For information address
Disney • Hyperion, 77 West 66th Street, New York, New York 10023.

First Edition, August 2023
10 9 8 7 6 5 4 3 2 1
FAC-004510-23181

Printed in the United States of America

This book is set in 13-pt Bulmer MT Pro, Latin MT Std, Southwest Ornaments MT, Fink
Condensed, Chesterfield LT Std, Grotesque MT Std, Courier New, Goldenbook, Itchy
Handwriting.

Designed by Alice Moye-Honeyman

Library of Congress Cataloging-in-Publication Data

Names: Curran, Kitty, author.
Title: Grave mistakes : a Dade family novel / by Kitty Curran.
Description: First edition. • Los Angeles : DisneyHyperion, 2023. • Series:
    Dade family • Audience: Ages 8–12. • Audience: Grades 4–6. • Summary:
    Twelve-year-old Molly and her poltergeist twin brother, Marty, must solve
    a mystery to protect their family.
Identifiers: LCCN 2022037966 (print) • LCCN 2022037967 (ebook) •
    ISBN 9781368083478 (hardcover) • ISBN 9781368097178 (ebk)
Subjects: CYAC: Twins—Fiction. • Brothers and sisters—Fiction. •
    Poltergeists—Fiction. • Blessing and cursing—Fiction. • Family
    life—Fiction. • Mystery and detective stories. • LCGFT: Detective and
    mystery fiction.
Classification: LCC PZ7.1.C86483 Gr 2023 (print) • LCC PZ7.1.C86483
    (ebook) • DDC [Fic]—dc23
LC record available at https://lccn.loc.gov/2022037966
LC ebook record available at https://lccn.loc.gov/2022037967

Reinforced binding

Visit www.DisneyBooks.com

SUSTAINABLE FORESTRY INITIATIVE
Certified Sourcing
www.forests.org
SFI-01681

Logo Applies to Text Stock only

To my family, for providing endless inspiration
when writing about weirdness

Chapter One

᎙

Molly Dade sat at her family's kitchen table and put on her thick welding gloves. Her violin case lay propped up against her clawfoot chair, taunting her. The audition for her school's Christmas concert was that afternoon, and she was doing her best not to think about it—just in case she threw up breakfast or something.

All around her, the sounds of her family filled the kitchen as they got ready for their day. And unfortunately for Molly, this included the sound of her sister, Dyandra, moaning from behind the stove.

Molly picked up Dyandra's mouth guard from the table, shoved it into her pocket, pushed up her glasses, and rolled her shoulders. She had spent every other morning since her family had adopted Dyandra wrestling the neon-pink mouth guard into her little sister's mouth. Seeing as that was nearly a year ago, you'd think Dyandra would have given up by now, but the kid was stubborn.

"Come on Dy-Dy," she crooned as she dropped to her knees and crawled around the stove. It was the tall, black, old-fashioned type, and lurked at the back of the Dades' kitchen about as spookily as it was possible for a kitchen appliance to lurk. Dyandra tried to make a break for the tall ebony cabinet next to it. From Molly's experience, if Dyandra made it up *there*, it would take at least three family members and something shiny to get her down. She wasn't going to let that happen. Molly faked going left, then used her right hand to grab her sister.

"AAARGH!" said Dyandra as she attempted to bite through Molly's welding gloves.

"Dyandra, sweetie . . ." Their mom floated over, her kaftan wafting on a breeze that Molly could not feel. Dyandra immediately calmed, though her mouth remained firmly clamped around Molly's hand. "Don't bite Molly. That's not nice."

"GAHHH," said Dyandra as she released Molly, pouting. Molly shook the feeling back into her hand. Her sister was deceptively strong for a three-year-old. She figured it was probably the zombieism.

"There's my sweet baby angel!" cooed their mom encouragingly. "That's right, Dy-Dy, open wide! We don't want you infecting anyone, do we?"

"Nuhhh." Dyandra sighed as she finally opened her mouth. Mom gave a round of enthusiastic yet silent applause.

"There we go, that's it, *quick, Molly, get it in*. . . . Okay, all done! Who's my good, clever girl?"

"Meeehhh!" Dyandra beamed through her mouth guard. Mom attempted to ruffle her hair. Her hand went slightly through Dyandra's head.

As Molly gingerly removed her Dyandra-spit-covered gloves, she felt her twin brother, Marty, rush into the room. "Morning . . ." he called as the chairs rattled. The homework assignment that was officially Molly's floated through the air onto the kitchen table.

In the year since the accident, Molly and Marty had split the work between them so that Marty could get at least *some* of his work graded without the school knowing. Molly was mostly grateful for the relief in her workload, but today she was especially glad she didn't have to do the project. It was a family tree, and while Molly had no issue with the upper branches, detailing Grammy Dade's ancestor who died at Gettysburg to Jia-Jia's parents' arrival from China in the 1950s, she could barely look at the lower branches.

Because there, written far more neatly than Molly's

own handwriting, was Marty's and Mom's death date. Molly shuddered and moved her chair away from the table. Across the kitchen, their dad looked up briefly from the now Dyandra-less stove where he was frying bacon. He held up a spatula.

"Hey, Marty, you up? Can you grab the eggs?"

Though she couldn't see them anymore, Molly *knew* Marty's eyes rolled at this. She'd tried explaining to Marty that it was like her mind was seeing what he was doing, even if her eyes weren't. They'd actually tested it, and Molly correctly guessed that Marty was jumping on one foot while tapping his head with his left hand and rubbing his belly with his right. After that, they'd decided it was probably a twin thing.

To make matters more complicated and also weirder, it seemed Marty and their mom weren't even the same *kind* of dead. After much searching on the stranger corners of the internet, the family had decided that Julia Dade was just a ghost—because she could be heard loud and clear by most people though she couldn't be *seen* by non-Dades. Marty, however, must be some sort of poltergeist—able to manipulate objects and electronics but unable to be heard by anyone outside the family.

Molly regularly wished it was the other way around, as disembodied voices tended to terrify people, and Mom was in the habit of forgetting this crucial fact. Molly knew that, for all his many, *many* annoying tendencies, Marty would probably handle this better.

Marty was not, however, handling Dad's request for eggs so well. Even in death, and with no body to slow him down, he still somehow managed to not be a morning person. Molly got up to save the picture that was now swinging precariously on the wall as her deceased brother stomped invisibly to the fridge.

Molly found herself hesitating as she straightened the frame. It was the last photo taken when everyone was still alive (well, apart from Dyandra, who was at that point still fully dead) at Christmas dinner last year. In it, Molly was seated between Marty and their dad, all as gangly as each other, with bodies that looked like they were made out of awkwardly bent coat hangers. Across the table sat Mom, her hair as black and messy as Molly's and Marty's. And next to her was their older brother, Timothy, tall, athletic, and grinning as goofily as ever.

Seeing images of her family like this always gave Molly a strange ache in her stomach. But like a scab you can't help scratch, she felt compelled to look at it more closely. Her fingers brushed on the image of her twin's still visible face for a moment before she forced herself to turn away.

Meanwhile, the fridge door opened as grumpily as possible and a carton of eggs drifted out. Molly managed to dodge it as she sat back down, but Mom walked straight through it on her way to kiss Dad.

It was Molly's turn to roll her eyes now. Mom had been spacey enough in life, but not having a corporeal form had only made matters worse. Dad didn't seem to care and accepted a phantom kiss from his wife as if she had been there in body as well as spirit. The egg carton appeared to land neatly in his hand. "Thanks, buddy. Hey, Tim!"

Timothy, the only other living Dade sibling, had entered the room grunting. His head was buried in his phone as usual. Dyandra grunted back enthusiastically as he high-fived her while still typing with one hand.

"Who're you texting?" asked Marty, his voice coming from behind Timothy's shoulder. Timothy didn't bother looking up to answer.

"Kaitlyn."

"Kaitlyn who?" Molly sighed, as she exchanged an invisible look with her twin. Timothy shrugged.

"Nguyen."

There was a brief moment of silence.

"You're texting Kaitlyn Nguyen?" squeaked Marty finally. Molly was fairly certain he was flailing his arms as he said it. "But . . . *how*?"

"Yes, and I dunno, she just asked for my number?" Timothy looked up, vaguely confused. An uncharacteristic frown formed on his face. "How do you know her? You're in sixth grade and . . . like . . . not alive."

"*Everyone* in Roehampton knows Kaitlyn Nguyen!" said Molly. "She's Miss Teen Maine!"

Timothy shrugged. "Kinda, second runner-up. But yeah, that's her." He turned back to his phone. "She's cool."

"Well, she sounds *lovely*," said their mom. Molly and Marty stared at each other (as much as they could).

"Why don't you invite her over some time?" asked their dad as he attempted to break eggs into the hot pan. He mostly succeeded.

"NO!" Molly was horrified. "Seriously, Tim, you *can't* let her see us when—"

Mom crossed her arms and frowned at Molly. "Look, I know we all decided to be careful, but there are limits, sweetie."

"Yes!" said Molly. "We *all* decided to be careful! Because if the wrong people find out *actual proof* of life after death, then half of you are probably going to spend the rest of your lives in experimental testing or something!"

"Technically speaking, wouldn't it be the rest of our afterlives?" said Marty.

"It doesn't matter!" said Molly. "What matters is we don't expose ourselves or get people talking!"

"Well, that's true, Moll," said Dad. "But we also talked about how it wasn't reasonable to tell *no one*."

"Exactly," said Mom. "So, if Timothy thinks Kaitlyn is trustworthy and can be let into the secret, then I think he should be fine to tell her!"

Timothy put his phone in his pocket and held up his hands.

"Guys, *guys*, seriously, we're just *texting*." He turned and grabbed his schoolbag while shoving a piece of toast in his mouth. "Anyway, I've gotta go. The guys from the team are picking me up."

As Molly watched her older brother bounce out of the kitchen, she wondered once again how he managed to be so well adjusted when . . . well, everything. She could see him from the kitchen window now, fist-bumping his friends before getting into the car. As if he didn't live in a creepy house in a cemetery, and as if half his family wasn't—

"You okay, sweetie?" asked her mom. Molly jumped. She didn't think ghosts could read minds, but Mom could be downright spooky when it came to sensing Molly's mood. She forced a smile.

"I'm fine, Mom."

Her mom frowned. "Okay, well . . . you just seemed really worried back there. And I know we all appreciate you looking out for us, but you shouldn't feel you need to hide everything."

"Mm-hm," said Molly, not liking where this conversation was going. Her mom put an arm around her shoulder and managed to mostly not go through her.

"I know you still haven't told Grace," said Mom. "And I do get that you're nervous. But she *is* your best friend and— Oh, also! Before I forget!"

Molly smiled for real this time as she followed her mom to the fridge. She had never been more grateful for her mother's tendency to get distracted. Mom pointed to a Tupperware container with a spectral hand. It was filled with pastries Molly had helped her make the night before.

"Could you bring the cheese rolls to the PTA meeting this evening? I'll meet you after school, and we can head over together."

"But, Mom—"

"Dad can't come to translate for me like he normally does. He's meeting the new assistant cemetery caretaker."

"Right, but, Mom—"

"Don't worry, I won't make you stick around—I know we've had that conversation. I just need you to take the cheese rolls. I'd bring them myself, but of course I can't carry them—"

"Yes, but, Mom!" shouted Molly louder than she

intended. "It's not like you can talk to the other parents if Dad's not there. Well, not without freaking them out anyway. So, you know, what's the point?!"

Molly immediately regretted saying anything. Her mom looked crushed for a moment before she stiffened her ghost spine.

"Now, just because there's not much I can do these days doesn't mean that I can't take an interest in my children's school," she said. "And just because I'm not alive doesn't mean the other parents won't want my famous cheese rolls!"

Molly sighed. She was about to relent out of guilt but was cut off by the chiming of their doorbell. She winced involuntarily. It was the old-fashioned type and sounded almost like a funeral toll. Molly and Marty often wondered if a previous cemetery keeper picked it out in order to scare off houseguests. Dad loved it. He always said it added "ambience."

"I think that's Grace and one of her dads." Molly grabbed the Tupperware from the fridge and her violin and homework from the table. "I'll bring the cheese rolls." She leaned in to kiss her mom goodbye as she always did and felt the icy air against her lips.

"Oh, thank you so much, sweetie," said Mom, smiling from ear to phantom ear, any hurt feelings forgotten. "And good luck with your audition! You've been sounding *wonderful.*"

"That's today?" said Dad, turning from the hot frying pan. "That's great! I'm sure you'll knock 'em dead, Moll!"

"Uh-huh. Yeah, thanks!" said Molly as she headed out of the kitchen, violin case, Marty's homework, and Tupperware clutched to her like a shield.

If they noticed anything wrong, they did not let on. Mom went back to fussing over Dyandra, and Dad back to ineptly frying eggs. Unfortunately, Marty was onto her.

"Nervous about the audition?" he asked as they walked past the stuffed skunk mounted to the wall of their foyer—a relic of Mom's taxidermy phase from when she was still alive. It pointed angrily to the front door, which was not only painted pitch-black but also featured skull patterns in the stained glass *and* a hand-shaped door knocker on the front. It matched the rest of the house, making it just the sort of creepy location that enticed teenagers to dare each other to knock and run. Which is exactly what they did before Timothy got cool.

"Yes, I'm a little nervous, and shh," whispered Molly, reaching for the door, balancing the Tupperware and homework against her violin case. When it came to Marty, there really wasn't any point in trying to lie. "We're nearly in public. Text only, or we'll look *weird*."

"Why? No one else can hear me," said Marty.

"Marty, come on!" hissed Molly. "I don't want to be

weird-staring-into-space-muttering girl. Not like last semester! Most people have stopped talking about that now, and I want that to continue." Molly bristled. Marty poltergeisted messages directly into her phone all the time, so she didn't understand what the problem was.

She could feel Marty roll his eyes again. "Fine."

"Thank you."

Molly's phone buzzed in her pocket as she opened the door, and she cast a look at where she knew he was smirking. She didn't have time to react any further, because she was immediately enveloped in the biggest of bear hugs.

"Molly, sweetie, how's it going?" Molly looked up. It was Dave, Grace's dad, who looked like young Santa, staring down at her sympathetically. Grace waved from behind her father. "And what are these?" he asked.

"Hi, Grace, hi, Dave. Um, these are cheese rolls. I promised my mom I'd bring them to the PTA meeting."

"*Molly!*" hissed Marty. Molly tried not to look in his direction, grateful once again it was only the Dades who could hear him.

"Umm . . . I mean I promised her I would bring them in . . . uh . . . remembrance?"

Grace and her dad nodded and gave her *that look*. The look everyone had been giving her in the year since the accident, a combination of pity and uncertainty at what to say next. It always made Molly feel especially guilty about not telling Grace the truth.

"I'm sure she would feel so proud of you," said Dave quietly as they walked past the tombstones to his SUV. Molly couldn't think of what to say to that, which was a problem because adults always interpreted her silence as quiet, tragic grief. This had gotten especially bad the past few weeks as December rolled around and the anniversary of Mom's and Marty's deaths approached. The fact that the accident had happened the day after Christmas only served to make everyone feel even more sorry for her, which Molly hated.

"Sooo . . . How's your dad doing?" said Dave overly brightly, clearly thinking the worst. This was going to be an awkward car ride.

"Good," said Molly. She opened the car door and allowed enough time for Marty to get in before climbing in herself. "He's obsessed with his new crematorium furnace. It comes from Denmark."

Dave turned to her as she sat down. Oh no, it looked like there were actual tears in his eyes.

"He's doing *such* a good job," said Dave. "Keeping it together after the accident. And then adopting your sister after finding her abandoned in the cemetery like that."

"Uh-huh," said Molly, looking down desperately at the cheese rolls as Dave started the car. She could see

Grace looking over at her from the corner of her eye.

"Dad, stop it. Molly doesn't want to talk about this."

"Oh gosh, I'm so sorry!" said Dave. "You must have noticed Ben and I love chit-chatting. It's why we gave up our accounting jobs to run a B-and-B! Our families couldn't believe we'd do something so wild, but we're free spirits!" Molly smiled weakly as Dave continued. "But anyway, I just wanted you to know that we are so proud of you all, and we're all looking out for you. Anytime you need us, not just rides to school. You know that, right, Molly?"

Molly nodded.

"Oh, listen to me blabber on. It must be strange for you being stuck in a car with such a kooky family!"

Molly looked back at her creepy house at the edge of the cemetery, at the charred remains of her mother's old art studio next to it, and at her invisible twin brother sitting next to her. Then she looked at Dave and Grace, in their nice beige car, and normal clothes, and normal lives.

"Mmm" was all she could think to say.

She checked her phone so that she didn't have to react anymore. Made you look, said the message from Marty.

Again, said the next message.

"Who're you texting?" asked Grace, peering over before Molly could stop her. She froze as she saw the screen with MARTY at the top.

"I . . . uh . . . just like to look at his messages sometimes," said Molly, desperately fumbling for an excuse. And Grace must have bought it, because tears started welling up in her eyes, too, and she gave Molly *that look* again.

"Oh . . . Molly," she whispered.

"Nice save," said Marty into Molly's ear. Molly kept her face as blank as possible and turned to gaze out the window. It was easier that way.

Chapter Two

"I am *so* sorry about my dad," said Grace, fiddling with her glasses nervously as they walked into school. The large redbrick building looked as neat as the kids filing into it and made Molly feel even more mismatched in her homemade clothes. She couldn't *wait* to grow out of them and refuse to help her mom sew any more.

"He really means well, but he just gets too involved sometimes," continued Grace. "And isn't so good with hints."

"It's fine," said Molly. "He's nice."

"Plus, he makes the best whoopie pies," added Marty. "Man, I miss those."

Molly tried her best not to look at Marty when he said this. "And anyway," she said over her brother, "we're all good. Dyandra's good, Timothy's good and also dating a beauty queen apparently, and Dad's so busy with work at the cemetery he's even hiring a new assistant."

"Oh, awesome!" said Grace. "I mean, not that the cemetery is busy, that's terrible, but, uh, the other stuff."

"Thanks!" said Molly as they walked through the classroom door. She didn't know what else to say, and apparently Grace didn't either, so they sat down at their desks in silence. It had been like this for a while with Grace. It was like every now and then they would forget how to be best friends and started acting like strangers who had to be nice to each other.

The weirdness lasted all the way through lunch, where they politely discussed their favorite TV shows, until the sixth period.

Their teacher, Ms. Lewis, made an announcement to the class. "Now I know everyone's gearing up for Christmas break," she said, smiling. "However, we will be working on a very special project next semester, and I want us to get a head start. You will all be divided into pairs at random. With your partner, you will research, design, and build a display based on the Roehampton witch trials."

While the rest of the class quietly squeed in excitement, Molly sank into her seat. She had spent most of her school career trying to dispel rumors about her family. Even before the accident, back when Marty was still alive, they were the weird kids. The kids with the wacky artist mom people said was a witch because of her clothes and art projects. And the cemetery keeper dad who wouldn't shut up about his creepy job. And the spooky house that everyone said was cursed.

In those days, Molly tried to shrug it all off, and do her best to appear normal. Timothy managed it, after all. She'd *almost* pulled it off. But then her mother's art studio had blown up, and aside from turning the Dades' lives upside down, the whispers about the cursed house became a lot harder to quiet.

In short, the whole class studying the lore surrounding her home for more than a semester was something that Molly very much did not want to happen. She turned and caught her archnemesis, Cara Hartman, smirking at her, expensively dressed and hair slicked back without a strand out of place as usual, like some preppy demon.

Ms. Lewis went on, "The winning project will eventually get displayed in Roehampton town hall, and the winning team will receive coupons to Ray's Lobster Shack. So, you know, high stakes. And I really want to make sure one of our teams beats the other classes'." Everyone giggled at this, including Molly. Ms. Lewis was her favorite teacher.

"So why are we doing this?" Ms. Lewis said, shaking

back her unruly head of curls. "Well, as you are probably aware by all the posters going up around town, we are coming up to the 350th anniversary of the Roehampton witch trials. Salem was the most famous, but there were witch hunts all over New England during this period . . . including one right here in Roehampton. The Roehampton trials are notorious for resulting in the only execution for witchcraft in Maine history—Mary Proxmire."

"I thought she was named Goody?" whispered Brayden Cartwright loudly.

Ms. Lewis nodded. "For those of you who are confused about all the Goody Proxmire signs and merchandise, 'Goody' was basically the old-timey version of 'Mrs.' Goody Mary Proxmire was just an elderly widow and midwife . . . before her own neighbors accused her of unholy acts."

"Like cursing Molly's creepy house!" called out Cara as the rest of the class laughed. Grace made sympathetic eyes at Molly, and Marty hissed a word he would not be able to say in class if anyone else could hear him. Molly winced back at Grace and ducked her head. *Of course* Cara wouldn't miss an opportunity to mess with Molly—they had hated each other since first grade after all.

However, to Molly's delight, Ms. Lewis turned and quietly stared down Cara. The rest of the class quickly silenced as Cara shuffled awkwardly in her seat.

"I want to make it clear—we are going to be studying *facts*, not superstition," said Ms. Lewis with a final pointed look at Cara. "This was a terrible time in American history, and it is important that we remember the past so that we don't repeat it. While Goody Proxmire was the only one convicted, over twenty people were accused at the Roehampton trials. Many of the families here are descended from them . . . as well from those who made the accusations. After our family tree assignment, some of you may even have discovered some connections to this time in your own family. Raise your hands if you know if you had any relatives involved."

Molly looked around. Several kids had raised their hands, including herself and, unseen by anyone, Marty. (Molly could hear the air whooshing past her.) She looked back at Ms. Lewis, who also had her hand raised.

"Yep, me too. My ancestor Isaiah Lewis was one of the seven people who accused Goody Proxmire of being in league with the devil. Those accusations, and the hysteria that followed, cost the poor woman her life." Then Ms. Lewis smiled wryly, suddenly no longer deadly serious. "Weirdly, I am *also* descended from Goody Proxmire on my mom's side. Funny how these things work out." The class giggled again, including Molly this time.

Ms. Lewis held up her hand to calm them. "So, as I explained, you will all be assigned pairs at random, courtesy of this spreadsheet I made. Once you hear your name, go line up with your partner. Then we'll all head to the library." The class looked around at each other warily as Ms. Lewis continued.

"First up is Grace Lee-Baker and Brayden Cartwright." Grace stood up and caught Molly's eye as she slumped toward Brayden's desk. He looked up for a second and belched. Molly winced at Grace, who made a pained face back. Molly chuckled; the nerves that had been plaguing her the whole day soothed a little. Because as bad as she felt for Grace, for that moment it was almost like things were normal between them again.

But the good feeling didn't last long.

"Molly Dade and . . . uh, Cara Hartman," said Ms. Lewis. Molly was shaken from her thoughts by the sound of the whole class making an involuntary "Oooh . . ." Cara pretended like she hadn't noticed and grabbed her violin case and bag. She made her way over to Molly, nose in the air.

Grace glanced at Molly, horrified. Molly raised her eyebrows back at her and sighed, doing her best to ignore Marty screeching "Oh, no WAY" next to her. Instead, she grabbed her own violin case, bag, and the Tupperware of cheese rolls, and walked over to meet Cara. Everyone in the class stared at them.

They continued staring as Ms. Lewis read out the rest of the pairs, and Molly and Cara studiously ignored each other. They didn't stop staring as everyone filed out of the classroom and into the computer room at the back of the library. They even kept staring and whispering to themselves as Molly and Cara settled in front of a computer. Molly began to feel like an animal at the zoo. She was determined not to give them a display.

"So . . . you raised your hand when Ms. Lewis asked if we had any family stories about the witch trials," Molly said, trying to keep her voice as boring as possible to discourage any eavesdroppers. Cara sniffed.

"So did you."

"Right," said Molly. "My mom's family, the Briningstools, were descended from Eliza Briningstool. She was accused of flying her broomstick to Kittery and back during the trials, with her twin brother, John Hotchkiss."

"Twins run in the family," filled in Marty.

"Twins run in the family," repeated Molly as Marty gave her an invisible thumbs-up. Cara frowned slightly.

"But wasn't your mom, like, Asian?"

Molly normally restrained an eye roll in situations like this but really couldn't be bothered to do so for Cara. "Her mom was Chinese, but her dad's family came here from England in the 1640s. That does happen, you know."

A few classmates giggled behind her, clearly enjoying the show. Annoyed, Molly immediately tried to make her expression and tone more neutral. "But yeah, I guess that means I'm related to *two* accused witches. How about you?"

"Reverend Ezekiel Hartman was my thirteen times great-grandfather," Cara said, shrugging.

Behind her, Molly could hear Marty groan, "Of *course* he was."

Molly, like Marty, knew enough about the witch trials from Dad's graveyard tours to goggle at Cara. "So . . . your ancestor was the main ringleader of the Roehampton witch hunt? And he accused my ancestors of being witches? And tried to get them executed?" She could hear a few of their classmates giggling again.

"Looks like it," said Cara, her face as bland as unbuttered toast.

"Awkwaaaaard . . ." said Marty in Molly's ear.

Molly ignored him and turned back to the computer. As she did, she felt her knees knock against something under the desk. Whatever it was fell and caused a series of loud clattering noises. Cara sniffed loudly at her.

Molly avoided her gaze and ducked under the desk. There, their straps tangled together, were Cara's and Molly's violin cases. Two physical reminders of the audition for the Christmas concert. The audition for the Christmas concert first chair that would take place immediately after this class. The one that she and Cara were both up for. Molly repressed a shudder. Instead, she squinted in the gloom and tried to separate the cases, banging her head under the desk as she did.

Rubbing her head and wincing, and ignoring another loud sniff that came from Cara's direction, Molly resumed fumbling over the straps. Finally separating them, she propped the cases back up as carefully as she could with hands that were annoyingly shaky. Cara's own shiny, well-cared-for violin case glowered at her in the darkness, making Molly's battered, sticker-covered case seem even shabbier than usual.

Cara had that effect in general, mused Molly as she clambered back into her seat. In addition to her abnormally neat hair, Cara's gray shirt and jeans were as creaseless as always. Molly didn't even want to think what she looked like next to her, with her battered boots, glasses that never sat straight, and shirt made out of something from the eighties that her mom had thrifted.

Molly sighed. It would be much simpler if she could just write Cara off as another spoiled rich girl who had great instructors. But the most frustrating thing about Cara was that she actually *was* smart, and she actually *was* talented. She was just also really mean. Molly had been trying, and often failing, to compete with her their entire school career.

"Uh, are you even listening?" Molly looked up to see Cara's large brown eyes flash, clearly annoyed.

"She was asking you if you had any ideas about how to

split the work," Marty whispered into her ear. Molly sat up straighter, and pretended to look insulted.

"Yes, actually," she said as primly as she could. "And I think it would be a good idea to divide the research in half, the victims vs. the accusers. So, you do one, and I do the other, and we put what we find together at the end to make the presentation."

"And what, you take the victims and I take the accusers? Because of our families? Is that what you're saying?" asked Cara, eyebrows raised.

"No, we can always do the other way around," said Molly with an exaggerated patience she hoped would needle Cara. "Whatever you want."

It seemed to work.

"It's fine," muttered Cara, refusing to look in Molly's direction. "Just make sure you actually do the work. I don't want you bringing down my grade."

"You too," said Molly. Cara sniffed again, then picked up her pristine violin case and bag, and stomped toward the back bookshelves. Half the class snickered and tittered among themselves as she did. Molly sighed and turned back to the computer.

Even though she no longer had to deal with Cara, the class seemed to drag as Molly's nervousness about the audition increased. The problem was that she couldn't predict how it would go when the time came. Sometimes, when Molly forgot her nerves, the music would take over her hands and arms, like they just somehow *knew* what to do. Like magic. In those times, music was the best thing in the world, almost like taking a break from her brain.

But other times, like *now,* where everything seemed to put Molly on edge, it felt like an invisible force was fighting against her and pressing on her violin strings, making the notes come out all wrong. And if *that* happened at the audition, then it would mean public humiliation, people laughing at her and talking about her, and—Molly could feel her head getting dizzy and her limbs tingling just thinking about it. She made her hands into fists and sat on them.

"Hey, Molly, are you okay?" asked Marty. Molly shook her head, and was about to reach for her phone when the bell rang. She was out of time for brooding. Instead, she grabbed her stuff, and braced herself.

She was halfway out the door when Ms. Lewis called her over. Molly winced and turned back. Ms. Lewis was, of course, giving her *that look.*

"Molly . . ." she said, "I know it must be hard. It's coming up to your first holiday season without your mom and your brother, and then the anniversary of . . . well. Anyway, you've been very mature about how you've handled this . . . but . . . I just want you to know . . . it's okay *not* to be. You know that, right?"

"Uh-huh . . ." said Molly, looking down at her feet.

She could feel Marty lean in to whisper to her. "Just tell her, Moll. Mom and Dad did say we could tell the people we could trust. And I trust her!"

Molly tried to ignore him and focus on her teacher.

"I know you are doing your best to be brave," said Ms. Lewis.

"Seriously, Moll, tell her!" said Marty. "This will make everything easier!"

"But I'm sure you miss them," continued Ms. Lewis.

"I could even give a poltergeist demonstration if you're worried she won't believe you!!" urged Marty.

"NO!" shouted Molly. Ms. Lewis blinked with surprise.

"I-I'm sorry?"

Marty burst into laughter next to Molly as she felt her face grow hot.

"I . . . uh . . . well I know that they wouldn't want me . . . to . . . have a bad Christmas?" she said desperately. "And I know they are still watching over me and Dad. And Tim and Dyandra. So, it's not like they are really, um, *gone*."

As Ms. Lewis glanced away for a moment, Molly took the opportunity to glare quickly in Marty's direction. He didn't stop laughing even slightly. To her dismay, when she turned back, Ms. Lewis seemed almost disappointed. This was somehow worse than *that look*.

"Oh, Molly, you know, you are a really brave kid," said Ms. Lewis quietly. "But you shouldn't feel you have to be strong all the time. It's okay to feel sad, and it's okay to need others sometimes."

"Right," said Molly.

"Just . . . if you ever need to talk, I'm happy any time, or I'm sure Grace would . . ."

"I know, Ms. Lewis . . ." said Molly, looking at the floor, wishing something would just make this all stop.

Just then, the main light in the room suddenly flickered and dimmed. Sparks flew as the room was cast into semi-darkness. As Ms. Lewis peered up at the ceiling, Molly saw a chance to escape.

"Sorry, I—uh—just need to get to the audition for the Christmas concert!" she said as she fled toward the door. "I'm up for first violin chair!"

And with that she ran from the room before Ms. Lewis had a chance to answer.

❧

Molly pulled out her phone in the hallway. Was that you? Messing with the lights? she texted Marty. She heard him chuckle next to her.

Yep, he messaged back.

As they got closer to the auditorium, they could hear a violin playing. It sounded beautiful. Molly felt the knot in her stomach tighten.

Thanks, she texted back. Feeling pretty nervous.

They entered the auditorium just in time to see Cara finish her audition. She smiled smugly as her friends in the audience and several teachers applauded and cheered. She caught Molly's eye, raised one eyebrow, then took a final bow. Molly swallowed and sat down next to Grace. Why couldn't Cara just be terrible at something for once in her life?

The rest of the kids who followed were mostly pretty good, but none even came close to Cara. Molly could feel her hands get sweaty and willed herself to think of anything other than how stressed she was. She wouldn't be able to play. Not like this.

"Last up, Molly Dade," said Mr. Anderson, the school music teacher. Molly felt the knot in her stomach tighten even more, then drop several feet. She made her way to the stage, hoping no one would notice her knees were shaking.

As she got up and took out her violin, the dizziness started up again, and the tingling in her hands. She flexed them one by one, forcing herself to take a shallow breath. The stage lights that reflected off the auditorium floor and Mr. Anderson's bald head seemed to flicker. It sounded like all the noise around her was coming from a tunnel.

"Molly! Moll!" Molly blinked at the sound of Marty's voice yelling into her ear. "Listen to me! Do you hear me? You've got this!"

Molly shook her head and stared at the ground, but Marty didn't stop.

"You are amazing! No, *better* than amazing! And you're Molly Dade! You've been practicing forever! All your hard work will pay off. I *know* it will."

Molly closed her eyes, less scared if only for a moment. She could feel it flicker inside—that feeling she got during those times when only she and the music existed. It was soft and barely there, but it was something. Enough to focus on, enough to believe it was real. She took a true deep breath this time and looked at where Marty was. Then she nodded, brought her violin to her chin, and lifted her bow.

And suddenly, it was one of those magical times. Molly's bow moved as if guided by something bigger than herself, and the music came out sounding exactly like she knew it would. This was why Molly played. Not for the compliments and praise—though those were nice. But for times like this. When the only things in the world were Molly, her violin, and the music.

The piece came to an end. Molly put her violin down and glanced up. It looked like Mr. Anderson had gotten to his feet and he was . . . applauding? Molly blinked and focused on the crowd. They were all standing and cheering, too. Well, apart from Cara Hartman and her friends. They were sitting, arms crossed, scowling at her. Molly smiled at them. That felt almost better than the applause.

"MOLLY! MOLLY! WOO!" cheered Marty as she stepped down from the stage. Mr. Anderson smiled at her.

"Well, I think it's safe to say we have found our violin chair for the Christmas concert! Congratulations, Molly Dade!"

As the cheers died down, Molly found her seat next to Grace, who hugged her. Mr. Anderson cleared his throat. "Before you all leave, I have some announcements to make."

Grace turned and whispered. "Hey, I'm going to get the last school bus—want to come with me?"

"I can't," said Molly. "Remember, I—" She paused as Mr. Anderson gave her a firm but kind look to silence her and continued talking.

"So now that we've officially cast all the roles for the Christmas concert, it's important you all bring your friends and *whole* families." Mr. Anderson adjusted his bow tie a little and coughed. "You should all know, the superintendent threatened to pull funding from the music program after barely anyone showed last time. Even after I created a new arrangement of 'Silent Night' especially for it, which neither the superintendent nor the school board seemed to notice. Apparently, musical innovation is not encouraged at Roehampton Middle School." Mr. Anderson's lower lip trembled, and an awkward silence fell over the room.

"But that's beside the point," he added, blinking quickly as he recovered. "It's crucial we have a good turnout for the concert this year. The music program needs you. This is all to say, I expect you to all bring at least *four* guests."

Molly groaned a little louder than the rest of the crowd. This was the last thing she needed, with only three living or semi-living family members. And who, in Dyandra's case, might not be trusted in a crowd filled with brains. Maybe she could pretend to be actually grief-stricken and tell Mr. Anderson that actually *none* of her family could make it, what with it being so close to . . .

Oh no. Molly noticed something out of the corner of her eye. There, standing at the far side of the auditorium, was the *actual* last thing she needed.

"Molly!" mouthed her mom from across the room, beaming at Molly and giving a dorky thumbs-up. Molly sighed and picked up the Tupperware as her mom waved at her manically, kaftan flapping, thankfully unseen by anyone but Molly and Marty.

"I gotta go," she said to Grace. "I'm bringing the cheese rolls to the PTA meeting."

Grace nodded. "Like your mom used to make. That

you promised you'd bring in her memory." She smiled at her like Molly had let her in on some kind of secret, which made Molly feel wretched.

"Uh. Yeah. That," Molly said, hurrying over to her mom. She tried not to think about how hurt Grace looked as she left.

Chapter Three

"O h, sweetie, I heard your whole audition," said Mom as they sped down the hallway to the spare classroom where the PTA met. "You were *amazing*."

"You were THE BEST!" whooped Marty.

"Shh . . ." hissed Molly, trying not to move her mouth. "We're almost there, and you know most people can hear you, Mom, even if they can't *see* you. Remember how much you scared the last mailman?"

"Oh, I'll be super quiet!" Mom whispered loudly. Molly could feel Marty's eyes rolling from behind her.

"Mom, I mean it," said Molly under her breath as she

opened the door. "Mrs. Grundy said he had a nervous breakdown! They had to give him a new mail route after he came back!"

Mom nodded, which was the best Molly could hope for. As they entered the room, she saw Grace's dads, Cara's mom and dad, and several other people who would be able to report any humiliation to her classmates. She sighed and braced herself.

"Oh, *Molly!*" gasped Grace's other dad, Ben, who was as skinny as Dave was large. "Are those the famous Dade cheese rolls?"

Molly nodded, a fixed smile on her face as she handed them out.

"You're the MVP, Moll, just like your mom," said Brayden's dad, his mouth already full of pastry. "And she was the best baker we had! You make these all by yourself?"

"Yes," lied Molly, keeping one eye on her mom in case she accidentally attempted to thank anyone. "I, uh . . . thought she'd want me to bring them like she always did."

This was clearly the wrong thing to say, as half the PTA's eyes immediately filled with tears. Molly hated playing the bereaved young girl at the best of times, and she couldn't help but feel extra gross when her mom and her brother were literally standing right next to her.

Fortunately, she didn't have to fake it for too long since

Dave strode over to give her another bear hug. "Oh, honey, I'm sure Julia's watching over you every time you make them," he said as he lovingly crushed her.

"Well, duh! She has to!" said Marty behind him. "Mom can't pick up stuff, and Molly can, like, burn water!"

"Marty, that's not nice," Mom said in a loud stage whisper.

"Did anyone hear that?" said Dave as he released Molly, frowning. Some of the other PTA parents looked around, confused. Molly shook her head, eyes wide.

Above them, the lights flickered. Sparks flew yet again. As Molly stared at the ceiling, she heard Marty say, "What? We needed a distraction!" Molly was once again very grateful that only she and Mom could hear him.

"Well, I guess we really should discuss the disgraceful state of this school building." Ben chuckled as he put his arm around Dave. "By the way, Molly, honey, I know Grace said she was getting the last school bus home and she's already left. Do you need a ride?"

"Oh, that would be—" said Mom before she stopped herself. Dave looked around again, as did several other parents.

"Okay, what *was* that?"

Molly shook her head and took the opportunity to back out of the door. The sooner she got her family out of public, the better.

"I'm fine but thanks!" The lights above them flickered and sparked some more. "So we—uh—*I* should get going. Now." Taking one last glance behind her, she saw the entirety of the PTA smiling at her sympathetically. And in the middle of them was her ghost mom, waving goodbye and mouthing, "See you at home." Molly sighed and backed out of the room with Marty right behind her.

As they left the school, Molly hoped her family didn't seem too weird to the PTA. Oh, who was she kidding? Dad normally went with Mom to translate her ghostly whispers into something that wouldn't terrify people. She didn't exactly trust either of them to make it look or sound natural. Molly cringed. She could only begin to think of what the other parents must be thinking about her dad and what they were telling their kids about him.

The walk home from school was only a mile, but the wind coming off the ocean made it seem much longer. A storm was brewing. Molly's ears and nose ached as she stomped down High Street, past the old pier and several seaside cafés.

"Come on, Molly, you crushed it today. And you got the part!" said Marty, his voice in her ear as they turned left at the old lighthouse. "So, what's the problem now?"

Molly sighed. She honestly wasn't sure. Any time her family had to interact with, well, *anyone* these days, she felt miserable. The other kids had living, breathing moms and siblings they could see. How could Molly not feel like a freak in comparison?

"Is this about the Christmas show? Are you panicking about *that* now?"

"No, don't be stup—" Molly stopped herself. In her alarm about seeing her mom at school, she hadn't thought more about Mr. Anderson's rule for their families to attend. Or the fact that Mom must have heard it, too.

"Oh," whispered Molly. "Oh no."

Several hours later, the Dades were gathered in front of the large fireplace in their main living room. The size of it and the way the strange carvings curved and twisted had always reminded Molly of the mouth of some monster, open and ready to devour. Tonight, it looked extra creepy, the flames licking and spitting like many tongues, and casting dark shadows across the room . . . and Molly's impending doom.

Mom was back from the PTA meeting, gushing about Molly's wonderful solo and the upcoming Christmas show. And once Dad heard, he of course was equally enthused. "That's great, Moll! We're all real proud of you."

"Aaargh!" said Dyandra.

"That's right, Dy-Dy," said Dad as he pulled her onto his lap. Dyandra started eating his sweater enthusiastically. "We can't wait to see Molly perform either!"

"Can I bring Kaitlyn?" said Timothy, keeping his gaze on his phone.

"Oh, that's a wonderful idea!" enthused Mom. "Molly's teacher said that she needed to bring as many people as she could. I think we should get there early so we can all sit in the front," she added cheerfully.

Molly could feel herself get dizzy, and pins and needles crept into her hands. She took a deep breath and attempted to gather herself. The fireplace seemed to roar even more intensely to taunt her.

"Guys, before you come to the concert . . . there's some stuff I want to go over with you. Like some ground rules. Please."

Not one of her family members seemed to notice. Timothy was still bent over his phone. Mom was discussing what she was going to bake for the concert with Marty, who was pretending to listen. And Dad was preoccupied bouncing Dyandra on his knee, who was throwing her hands in the air and exclaiming "Yeeeaarggh!" with delight.

"GUYS!" Molly screamed. Her family immediately turned and stared at her, which made her feel small and guilty. She quieted her voice. "Look, I'm glad you are excited. But we really need to make sure we don't expose ourselves at the concert. So, first off, we need to put makeup on Dyandra to make her less . . . green. Are you okay with that, Dy-Dy?" Dyandra grunted and nodded, then went back to eating Dad's sweater.

"Okay . . . good. And, Mom? I know Dave and some of the other parents heard you *twice* tonight. You are supposed to be *dead*, and seeing as most people outside the family can't see you, hearing a voice without a person will freak everyone out. You really need to stay quiet, okay? You and Marty *have* to keep yourselves hidden."

Mom floated down several inches, head hanging. "I understand, sweetie," she said quietly. "It's just that I really miss talking with the other parents. I admit I didn't really socialize with the PTA outside of school when I was alive . . . but I *know* I will want to gush about how wonderful you play with, well, pretty much everyone . . ."

"I have an idea, Julia!" said Dad to Mom, suddenly animated. Even Dyandra looked startled. "Why not use one of the bodies waiting for burial? Just for the concert. We have an out-of-towner due to be buried two days after, so we won't have to worry about anyone recognizing you! We could pass you off as a cousin visiting for the holidays."

"Oh, Jeremy, you are so smart!" said Mom as she planted a ghost kiss on Dad's cheek. He looked pleased. "That is a *genius* solution! And we can just return the body at the end of the night!"

Molly stared at her parents and their newfound excitement for body snatching. Passing even the living Dades off as normal was probably going to be harder than she thought. Still, Mom was so excited at the thought of getting to talk to anyone outside the family, Molly didn't have the heart to stop her.

"Okay, *fine*." She sighed. "Mom will possess a body. But you need to practice possession ahead of time, Mom. You've only done it once and that was by literally tripping and falling into a body by accident." Molly shuddered. "And you didn't seem exactly in control when you did it that time."

"Poor Mr. Nutter," said Mom, shaking her head sadly. "I hope I didn't damage his body too much."

"Right," said Molly, trying desperately to keep her voice even. "Exactly. And if you have an accident again, or worse, slip out during the performance . . ."

"Oh, of course! Jeremy, do you have a few bodies I can practice on in the meantime?" said Mom.

"Sure thing, honey!" said Dad. "And I'll make sure to lay some cushions down first."

"Perfect! Oh gosh, I can't wait!" Mom spun around where she was floating, and even Molly smiled despite herself. She turned to Marty.

"Marty, you can't move things or scare people. Yes, even

if I need a distraction—I appreciate you helping, but you pulled the light thing *twice* today; people are going to start noticing this only happens around me."

She felt Marty slump in his chair.

"Fine," he said. "But don't blame me if you change your mind."

"I definitely won't," said Molly. "And one last thing. Dyandra?"

"Yuh?" said Dyandra.

"No eating brains. Or even trying. Even if there is a dog that looks really tasty. Eating pets will upset the owners, Dy-Dy, and give us all away."

"Muhhh." Dyandra pouted and crossed her arms, but she didn't look like she disagreed. Molly took that as good enough.

"But seriously, can I bring Kaitlyn?" asked Timothy, looking up from his phone to make his point. "I know she'd get a kick out of it. She was the first violin chair her whole way through Roehampton Middle School."

"Of course she was," muttered Molly to herself. Timothy carried on, oblivious.

"She also did violin as her talent when she did Miss Teen Maine. She only applied to the pageant so she could win enough money to go to Juilliard." He smiled back at his phone and resumed texting.

Molly stared at her living brother for a few seconds before giving up. "I . . . Fine. Timothy can bring his beautiful talented girlfriend to witness my humiliation, too."

"She's not my girlfriend, we're just hanging ou—" said Timothy before he was cut off by the doorbell. Molly winced as the clanging chimes rang throughout the house, somehow even more doom-laden than usual. The thunder and lightning that suddenly started at the same time did not help.

Dad jumped up. "That'll be Mr. Bones, the new assistant caretaker! I said I'd show him around our house after dinner. He seems like a bit of a history nerd—wanted to know all about the building." Dad chuckled to himself as he left the room.

Molly fell silent. The rules her family had agreed to were probably the best she could manage. Her thoughts were suddenly interrupted by the sound of Marty gasping loudly. Which made no sense, as he didn't have lungs. She turned and frowned at her brother, but his attention was on the door.

Molly followed his gaze and almost gasped herself. For there, looming in the darkness of their entranceway, drenched to the skin, was the single spookiest man she had ever seen. His dark eyes glanced around the Dades' admittedly shabby foyer, as blank and glassy as the eyes of the stuffed and mounted animals that decorated it. His skin was so pale and lifeless, it looked as if he had been left underwater for a long time. And his long black coat, which was dripping wet from the rain, only added to the drowned-man look.

"Wow," whispered Marty. "That guy looks like he's from a horror movie!" If he still had ribs, Molly would have elbowed him in them.

"Hello, Jeremy," said the spooky man in an unearthly British monotone. "I hope I'm not . . . interrupting."

"Huh," whispered Timothy back to Marty. "He *sounds* like he's from a horror movie, too. Cool."

"Shuddup, both of you," hissed Molly. The spooky man was looking directly at them.

"Bones!" Dad said as he reached to take the man's coat, cheerful as ever. "Glad you could make it! I'll give you the full tour, but first you should meet everyone! Kids, this is Mr. Bones, my new assistant."

Both living and almost-living Dades shuffled forward. Mr. Bones remained as motionless as a tombstone, staring at the family wanly. He didn't even start when a loud crack of lightning caused everyone else to jump.

Dad let out another chuckle. "This is Timothy, my eldest. He's the one who's in all the basketball photos in the office."

"Hey," said Timothy smiling, sounding almost as unfazed as Dad.

"And this is Molly, who had the violin audition I was

telling you about," said Dad, pointing to Molly and smiling proudly. "You did great, didn't you, Moll?"

"Y-yes," said Molly, not taking her eyes off Mr. Bones.

"And this is my youngest, Dyandra. Say hello, Dy-Dy."

"Heaaargh!" said Dyandra, running to hide behind Dad's legs. Molly wished she was young enough to get away with doing the same.

"Do you think he's . . . one of us?" Marty whispered in her ear. "I mean, he kinda looks . . . not living."

"Is there someone else here?" said Mr. Bones, looking around. "It sounded a bit like . . . a young boy whispering."

Molly stopped her jaw from dropping just in time. Next to her, Marty seemed thankfully too surprised to make any further noises. Even Dyandra kept quiet.

"Whoa, that's amaz—" said Timothy, not even attempting to hide his shock. Molly silently thanked the universe that *this* brother still had ribs as she elbowed him in them.

"*Ow!*" squawked Timothy before he looked at all of his siblings, living, dead, and semi-dead (or as much as he could in Marty's case). As they glared at him, realization dawned on his face. "Oh. Yeah," he mumbled, before finally shutting up.

"Well, let me show you around!" said Dad, leading Mr. Bones away. He motioned to follow him down their long ominous hallway. "So, this version of the house was built in the 1890s—"

"Ah, that explains the Victorian Gothic revival exterior with the art nouveau, almost Gaudí-esque interior," said Mr. Bones, walking behind Dad like an extra shadow. "A transitional style, you might say."

Dad made the face he always did when he pretended to understand something. "Exactly! But a house has stood on this spot since the 1660s, you know. This is the sixth one so far . . . some say the land itself is *cursed*."

"Fascinating," drawled Mr. Bones as they disappeared down the hall. Molly sighed. Mr. Bones was admittedly terrifying, but she had something far scarier lurking on the horizon. She shuddered, grabbed her violin case, and headed to her room. The more practice she could get in before the Christmas concert, the better.

Whatever music magic had found Molly earlier that day was gone. As she drew her bow against the strings and tried to find any spark hiding inside, strange angry squeaks were all that came out. Molly adjusted her bow and tried again. This, if anything, made it worse. It was like the strings were *mad* at her, and she was *mad* at them, and they had both decided to go to war against each other.

Molly put down her violin, rubbed her eyes, and groaned.

Why was she even worrying about her family? The way she was playing, she'd embarrass herself anyway. What else could go wrong?

The dizziness was back now, too. Molly took a shaky breath and picked up her phone. She *had* to get out of her weird house, her weird family, and her weird life.

"Moll, are you okay? What's wrong?" asked Marty as Molly fled from her room. The lights trembled and flickered as she pushed past him.

"Not now, Marty, I mean it," said Molly. Marty, for a change, was one of the last people she wanted to be around. How was she meant to explain to him that one of her biggest problems right now was his current lack of life without hurting him? "I just need to be alone for once!"

That came out harsher than she intended.

"Fine," Marty muttered as he stomped back into his room. He slammed the door, and Molly winced before heading outside.

As she wheeled her bike out of the garage and texted Grace, Molly didn't even feel slightly better. Sure, she could talk to Grace about preconcert jitters, or perhaps a little about how much Dad's new co-worker was creeping her out, or maybe some of why she was not happy about everyone in their grade doing a project related to the curse on her creepy house.

But the big stuff? The fact that, despite the fact her mom and brother were dead, they were still there? And that her little sister was also, technically, dead? And even though her parents had told her several times that she could tell Grace, Molly just hadn't been able to come up with the words to explain ... *everything*? And that maybe now someone outside their family could understand Marty and blow their cover?

All those problems? Those she had no one to talk to about.

Molly fought back tears for the first time in months. She rubbed her eyes roughly with her sleeve, put on her helmet, and got on her bike. Grace's house was only a block away, and she had already texted Molly back. The storm had cleared, but as she cycled the familiar route, Molly couldn't help but feel a lingering chill creep down her neck.

Chapter
Four

A few minutes later, Molly pulled up to the charming seaside bed-and-breakfast run by Grace's dads. It towered over Molly, but in a quaint way—like some sanitized, edited-for-TV version of Molly's actual house of horrors. It was also supposed to be haunted (or at least that's what they told the guests), but as far as Molly and Marty could tell it was definitely not.

The bell for the door rang as Molly entered. "Just me!" she called out. Ben waved to her from the front desk. He was talking with two customers, a cool-looking young couple who seemed to be just checking in, judging from their bags and the lecture on Roehampton he was giving them. The woman of the pair leaned casually against the edge of the desk, the sleeve of her leather jacket riding up to show a delicate geometric tattoo. She cocked an almost interested look in Molly's direction before turning back to Ben.

"So, as you may be aware, Roehampton is known as Maine's Most Haunted Town," Ben was saying, "and 'most haunted' for Maine really is saying something!"

The couple laughed politely.

"Yeah, we passed through last year, saw all the signs, and knew we *had* to come back," said the man. "We're definitely hoping to see some spooky stuff while we're here."

"Well, you've come to the right place!" said Ben, smiling. "I'm sure you and your wife will experience at least one strange thing while you're in town."

"Oh, God, no, Ethan's my brother!" said the woman as she chuckled and shook her head. "I have *much* better taste in men than that!"

"Oh, I am *so* sorry," said Ben, looking mortified.

"No worries, it happens a lot. We travel together all the time, and everyone assumes since both our last names are Weston . . ." said the woman. "Our mom was really into supernatural stuff, so we take a trip once a year in her memory to go ghost hunting. Plus, we have a paranormal-themed podcast ourselves now, so this is all great research, too!"

Molly shuddered. While this was normal for tourists, she was still extra glad Marty was not with her this evening, near any ghost-hunting equipment that could expose them. She pretended to study the nautical themed art on the walls as she waited for Grace, hoping she looked normal as she listened in on their conversation.

"Mom died right around this time of year," continued the man, who thankfully hadn't looked her way. "So we try to honor her memory and make it through the holidays by doing exactly what she loved best. It's what she would have wanted."

"I'm so sorry for your loss," said Ben.

"Thanks, but it happened a long time ago. When we were kids. So, you know, we've had a lot of time to process." The woman grinned. Ben smiled nervously, clearly relieved at not having upset the customers.

"Well, I'm happy to hear that. That you're good, I mean," he said. "Ahem. So, ah, if you are looking for ghosts, we *are* in direct sight of the old lighthouse. It's said to be haunted by the ghost of a former lighthouse keeper. Legend has it that he used to deliberately turn off the signal so that ships would sail into the cliffs nearby. Then he and his gang would head to the shore and loot the wreckage . . ."

"Hey Molly!" called out Grace as she came down the stairs, juice box in one hand. Molly waved at her.

"They say his ghost still walks the tower every night, turning on the light to atone for his sins and find a way to salvation!" Ben continued, really getting into it. "My husband, my daughter, and I have all seen the lighthouse turn on by itself *so* many times . . . when not a soul should be in the building. Or not a *living soul* that is . . . Isn't that right, Grace?"

"Yes," said Grace, a little less spookily than her dad. "And so has Molly."

Molly shrugged. "I mean, most people in Roehampton have. . . . It happens a lot. I think there's something wrong with the wiring in the building."

"Molly here is a skeptic," said Ben, raising his eyebrows in amusement. Molly smiled politely.

"Cool," said the woman, grinning at her. Despite herself, Molly couldn't help but feel a little pleased.

"Then there's the haunted college, the haunted museum, and the cursed *and* haunted cemetery. Where Molly lives!" Ben looked winningly at Molly. This was a cue for Molly to chime in with her take on the tale, which every single other Dade loved to do (including Mom and Marty back in the day). It was almost like they were *proud* of their dumb creepy house.

"Dad, don't . . ." said Grace.

Molly knew why Grace was nervous. Even before the accident, Molly would normally sigh and run through the story as quickly as possible, making it very clear that she didn't believe *any* of it. Which was admittedly harder to do in the past year, but she still tried.

Strangely though, Molly didn't have the urge to do that this time. She felt oddly comfortable around this pair. Maybe it was because they were brother and sister, like an older, edgier, still-living version of her and Marty. Maybe it was because they also had their lives messed up when they were young around the holidays. Maybe it was just because she liked that people who were older and cooler seemed to think that her life was interesting, too.

"Yeah, my dad's the cemetery keeper," Molly started. "And, like, the old cemetery keeper back during the Roehampton witch trials was one of the main accusers of Goody Proxmire. She was the only person that got executed."

"We have a pamphlet all about the Roehampton witch trials if you want to read up," said Ben, handing over a leaflet with a cartoon witch on it.

Molly continued her story. "And since the town thought she was a witch, they wouldn't allow her to be buried in the cemetery. So she's buried under an old hawthorn tree just outside, on unhallowed ground, which was apparently a big deal. Because of that, and because the cemetery keeper accused her, she supposedly cursed the entire grounds. Which is where I live now."

Ben must have realized where this story was heading, as he suddenly looked worried.

"Molly, honey . . ."

"Oh, it's okay, Ben. It's a good story, even if I don't believe it," said Molly. The cool brother and sister still looked interested in everything Molly had to say. "People around town believe in the curse because my house has been rebuilt, like, six times. It's been burned down mostly, though one time it was hit by a hurricane and *then* burned down."

"Awesome!" The woman laughed. Molly glowed inside, but tried to grin casually back.

"Yeah! The house I live in now nearly burned down in the fifties, and then again in the nineties, but firefighters were able to save it. But then my mom's art studio, which was in the old crematorium, exploded last year."

Grace glanced back at Molly, her eyes worried. Molly smiled and shook her head. These two guests had gone through something similar. She felt they wouldn't be weird about the accident.

"Some say Goody Proxmire's curse extended to the whole town," said Ben, quickly trying to change the subject.

"Yeah, Dee and I heard about some of that," said the man. "Like strange noises coming from the cemetery . . ."

Molly winced and thought of Dyandra. "Um, yeah, I've

heard some stuff." She shrugged. "But I think it's just raccoons."

"Oh, and weren't the ducks in the local pond found with their brains missing earlier this year?" said the woman.

"Maybe . . . rabid raccoons?" said Molly, trying very hard to keep her expression blank.

"The one we were *really* interested in was that rain of frogs at the high school basketball game," said the man. "We read about it when we were researching our trip to Roehampton."

"Oh, you were at that game, weren't you, Molly?" said Grace, clearly happy to talk about something else. She probably thought the memory was less painful for Molly. It was not.

The frog shower had happened before the accident. Mom and Marty were both still alive. She remembered the look on Marty's face after a frog landed on him, and Mom as she laughed and tried to take a photo. She'd been so annoyed with them that day, because they had all seemed so *embarrassing*. And then Timothy's team was playing horribly, which she *knew* would make him grumpy, which she was really not in the mood to handle. . . . She'd just been so *angry* at everything. And that anger seemed so dumb now, because she would have given anything to have her family back. Back to exactly the way they were that day when everything they did seemed to embarrass her.

Molly blinked, swallowed, and forced herself to smile. "Yeah, it interrupted the big game. My brother Timothy was playing, like *really* badly. He said he was actually relieved about the frogs 'cause they had to cancel the game."

"Did they ever find out what happened?" said the woman. "It's not every day you get showers of frogs . . . let alone inside."

"I think they said they took shelter in the rafters or something. And then the cheers of the crowd dislodged them," said Molly. "But yeah, it was freaky."

"And wait until I tell you about what happened to me and my husband on our first date at the haunted museum . . ." said Ben, leaning over the front desk. The cool brother and sister turned their attention to him. Molly looked at Grace and pointed to the door. She needed to get out now.

Grace nodded and waved to her dad. "I'm just headed to the beach with Molly."

"Bye, honey, have fun!" said Ben before turning back to his guests. "And the only parts of the museum curator that they found . . . were his *feet*!"

Molly and Grace headed to the beach in silence. It looked like Grace kept trying to say something before stopping herself. Across the bay, the lighthouse sent thin beams out into the early evening light.

"Um . . . so . . . the light's on again," said Molly, grateful for the topic of conversation. "Your dads' new guests will be pleased."

"What? Oh, uh, yeah. That's good." Grace frowned, before taking a deep breath. Molly felt the pins and needles in her hands again and flexed them desperately.

"Look, Molly," Grace said after what seemed like an eternity. "I've been meaning to talk to you. I know you've been going through a lot. And I get it."

"Do you?" said Molly. For the second time that day, she realized that that had come out harsher than she had intended. Grace didn't storm off like Marty, but she looked hurt. Which, if anything, felt even worse. The prickling feeling crept up Molly's neck.

"Um, I guess not," said Grace, fiddling with her glasses and then her sleeves. "But what I mean is . . . it's understandable given, you know, *everything,* that you've been acting strange this year."

"I've been acting strange?" said Molly, much louder than she meant to. Grace frowned again.

"Well, no, not *strange.* But we used to tell each other *everything*, and now half the time it's like you're thinking all this stuff, but you're not telling me. And it's not like you should feel you have to, but it looks like it's making you upset—"

"I am NOT upset," said Molly, trying to ignore the tears that were forming in her eyes. The wind chose precisely then to pick up and blew them in obvious watery streaks across her face. Molly blinked furiously.

"Okay, no, not upset," said Grace. "But, um, you don't seem yourself. And I just wanted you to know, I'm here for you if you ever want to talk—"

Molly finally snapped. She spun around, her hair blowing wildly in the wind.

"What is there to say? My mom converted the old crematorium into a kiln for her art studio, it wasn't up to code, and it blew up on her and my brother? And now my life will never be the same?"

Grace tried to put her arm around her. "Molly . . ." And even though Molly had a feeling she would regret this later, she threw Grace's arm off and stormed off in the other direction.

"Forget it," she yelled back at Grace over the wind that was howling almost as loudly as she was. "I just want things to be *normal*. And they *never, ever are*. And they *never, ever will be*."

Molly grabbed her bike, put on her helmet, and took off. She couldn't let her family see her like this. Not with tears running down her face. Because then they would ask questions, and she wouldn't know what to say to them, or how to not cry or scream her answer if she did. She took several trips up and down the beach bike lane before she felt calm enough to go home.

It was already dark by the time Molly got back. As she hopped off her bike she spotted her dad and Mr. Bones in the cemetery, standing around an open grave. Her dad was waving his arms excitedly, which meant he was either on the topic of traditional gravestone motifs, fly fishing, or the latest furnace that had been installed in the new crematorium. (Thankfully, this one was located on the other side of the graveyard, far from the house.) Mr. Bones was nodding politely.

"Hey, pumpkin!" called out Dad. "How's Grace?"

"Hey, Dad! She's good," lied Molly. "Evening, Mr. Bones."

Mr. Bones nodded at her, not blinking once.

Molly felt a chill run down her spine and rushed back into the house.

Chapter
Five

❧

Three weeks, twelve rehearsals, and multiple forced partnerships with Cara passed. It was now judgment day—the night of the big Christmas show.

Molly paced backstage, too stressed to feel any holiday cheer. She tried to take deep breaths and hoped she didn't appear too nervous to her classmates. Hearing a giggle behind her, she looked to see Cara whispering something into her friend's ear. Cara's friend glanced at Molly, then laughed even louder.

Molly hunched her shoulders and took a peek behind the curtain at the waiting audience. To her surprise, her family looked . . . actually *not bad.* In fact, in their new clothes, new makeup (and in one case, new body), they could almost pass as any other normal family in the crowd. Some high school kids and their parents high-fived Timothy for his latest win. He grinned, the radiant Kaitlyn sitting next to him, looking far too beautiful for the audience of a middle school concert.

Next to her, her mom waved shyly to Ben and Dave and they . . . looked confused, but then started waving back. Dyandra sat on Dad's lap, makeup and neon-pink mouth guard on, and a doll missing the top half of her head in her arms. Molly breathed a sigh of relief. Maybe this would go better than expected.

She yelped as she felt someone tap her shoulder. Steadying her breath, she turned and saw Grace.

"I wanted to wish you good luck," Grace said. She looked just as uneasy as she had the past few weeks since their big argument.

"Oh, thanks!" said Molly. She leaned in to hug Grace, but Grace leaned the same way. She changed direction just as Grace did, and finally stood still as Grace put her arms around her. Molly hugged her back because she was meant to, but it felt weird. She had apologized to Grace several times, and Grace accepted her apology several times (much quicker than Marty had when Molly had also apologized to him).

But even after all that she still felt . . . not as close with her friend. They were back to acting like polite strangers who were forced to hang out together, except that it was all the time now.

"Places, everyone, curtain's about to go up!" called out Mr. Anderson, wringing his hands. Molly's stomach lurched, and she gripped Grace tighter. Grace giggled and hugged her back, genuinely this time, which almost made Molly feel better.

"Don't worry," said Grace. "You'll be great, I know it." Molly nodded back shakily. She picked up her violin and headed to her chair.

The curtain rose, and the audience clapped politely. Molly tried to look again for her family, but the lights were blinding her eyes. Her mouth felt dry, her palms sweaty. The tingling was moving up and down her whole body, not just her limbs, and the dizziness in her head now combined with a ringing in her ears. She blinked, took in one breath that came in all ragged and shallow, and stood up. Her knees were shaking, and she was certain that everyone could see.

She put the violin to her chin and her bow to the violin. "Please, please, please," she whispered to herself and the music, willing just a little bit of that magic from that day of the audition to return to her.

It did not.

Instead, what came out was a long, hollow screech, louder and harsher than anything Molly had made with her violin before. A few people in the crowd giggled nervously, and Molly's face got hotter and hotter. She took another raggedy breath and tried again.

This time the violin sounded like it was being dragged against a chalkboard. There were even more giggles. Molly wished she hadn't ordered Marty to stay in the audience. She wished even more that Timothy hadn't brought a classical violinist as his date to witness this.

Molly lifted her bow one more time. She had played "God Rest Ye Merry Gentlemen" a million times before; she could do this. She closed her eyes, took one more deep breath and—

One of the strings broke. Molly stared down at her violin, one string now dangling uselessly as an awkward silence filled the room, even more terrible than the giggles and the screeches before.

But then—music. Beautiful music, and not coming from Molly's bow. She turned and saw Cara Hartman, smiling smugly, playing Molly's solo one hundred times better than Molly ever could. Cara looked Molly in the eye and raised one eyebrow.

Molly felt her breath quicken and her head spin. She had just changed those strings! Could Cara have sabotaged her?

She stared at Cara, who was still playing, now looking sweetly at the audience. Around her, the rest of the band started to nervously join in, before gradually hitting their stride. They actually sounded *better* than in rehearsals.

And all the while Molly stood in the middle of them, looking like an *idiot*. Her hands balled into fists so tight she could feel her nails digging into her palms. She hated Cara, that *witch*!

Above her, the lights started flickering. *Oh no, Marty . . .* thought Molly as she tried to desperately find her brother in the audience to signal him to stop. The crowd shrieked as a shower of sparks rained down from one bulb before it finally exploded.

The band, even Cara, stopped playing and stared. Behind her, Molly heard a cymbal crash. She turned and stared at Brayden, who was shaking his head at everyone, hands up and away from his cymbal, which was swinging wildly back and forth by itself. Suddenly someone in the audience screamed. Molly spun around and saw why.

In her shock, Molly's mom had left her borrowed body. She was actually floating up toward the stage, up toward Molly, arms outstretched to comfort her. Which did *not* comfort Molly, because if she was not in her body, then—

Someone else screamed out from the audience. "Oh my god, I think she's DEAD!" Molly didn't have time to react because she could see Dyandra, groaning and crashing through the audience after her mom. Her flesh-colored makeup was getting rubbed off in the ruckus, exposing the green lifeless skin beneath. Meanwhile she could hear her dad yelling above it all, "Nothing to worry about, folks, my cousin's just *really tired.*"

A louder sound clanged behind her, and the rest of the audience started screaming. Molly turned to see the school piano flying through the air. Not far, or very high, admittedly, but enough to turn it on its side with a massive CRASH. Molly started to panic. This had gone too far, even for Marty. What was he thinking?

She had to stop him. Somewhere, out in the crowd, he was there, causing this. Molly ran to the front of the stage and screamed.

"MARTY, STOP!"

Immediately the lights stopped flickering, the cymbal stopped swinging, and the piano . . . was still on its side, but at least it wasn't moving anymore. Even Dyandra and Mom stopped what they were doing. But as Molly looked down at the audience, she saw something worse. Something, in all of Molly's potential worst-case scenarios, she had not thought of.

There, seated in front of her, were one hundred people. All giving her *that look.*

Then the lights cut out.

Molly gasped and fled. She ran out from backstage, down the hallway, and out through the back door of the school without once looking behind her. She could never go back. Not after this.

"Molly, wait!" called out Marty behind her. Molly refused to stop and kept running out past the school gate.

"Molly, listen to me!" yelled Marty. Molly kept running. She did not want to listen to her brother, not when he had just ruined her life. Ahead of her, the ocean sparkled and glinted. The lighthouse was out, and only an almost-full moon lit the sky. Molly felt the sand fill her sneakers as she hit the beach, but she didn't slow down.

"Moll, you don't understand!" shouted Marty, closer to her now. Molly had finally had enough.

"Oh, *I* don't understand?" she shouted back at the empty space behind her. "I specifically told you *not* to do any poltergeist stuff, and what do you do?"

"But—"

"NO. I'm talking! I just wanted my life to be normal, but none of you listen, and none of you ever understand! Do you think after tonight I'm ever going to have friends? That I'll ever get another solo? That I'll ever be able to show my face in school again?"

Marty made a strange sound that was almost a sob. Molly stopped in her tracks.

"No, Moll, you don't understand," he said, his voice trembling. *"It wasn't me."* Molly stared at where her brother was hovering. She knew that if she could see him, he would look terrified.

"What?" she whispered. She felt Marty shake his head.

"I mean, I stayed in my seat literally the whole time. I swear, Molly, it wasn't me messing with the lights, the cymbal, the piano . . . any of it."

Molly had that cold prickly feeling up her spine, the type you got just before you realized something horrible. Marty's whole being was shaking now.

"And if it wasn't me doing those things . . ." he whispered. *"Then who was it?"*

Chapter
Six

"**B**ut you homeschool Dyandra!" yelled Molly to her parents. It was Sunday evening, and despite almost a whole weekend of arguing, they hadn't budged.

"That's because she's a zombie, sweetie," said her mom. "You're a living girl, and it's important for you to have meaningful interactions with your peers."

"Heeeh," said Dyandra, far too smugly for a three-year-old.

"Besides, if I remember middle school," said Dad, "everyone will be over it by now!"

"Then you DON'T remember middle school!" screamed Molly.

"I really don't think you have anything to worry about,"

said Mom. "The school appeared to chalk it all up to some 'technical difficulties.' Besides, it's the last week before Christmas break and most people are focused on more festive matters anyway."

"Like the decorations I've hung up around the cemetery!" said Dad. "The headstone Advent calendar has all the neighbors talking!"

"That's not a good thing!" Molly's head spun. She didn't think she had ever been so frustrated in her life. Above her the lights flickered. Mom looked up and sighed.

"Oh, Marty." She sighed. "He really has been acting out all weekend."

"Uh, maybe that's because *none of you believe him*," said Molly, fuming on her twin's behalf.

"Now, Molly," said Dad sternly. "We do believe Marty when he says he didn't do anything on *purpose*. . . ."

"But when you remember how empathetic Marty is, then combine that with his supernatural powers and puberty making everything ten times worse . . ." added Mom.

"Mom!" screeched Molly, throwing her hands over her ears. Dad put a supportive arm around Mom, or as much as he could anyway.

"I'm just saying, let's be realistic here. I'm sure Marty means it when he says he wasn't *aware* he was throwing the piano at anyone, but . . ."

"Well . . . who else could it be, honey?" finished Mom.

The lights flickered above them again.

Mom sighed again. "Though I do think it would be a good idea to check in on him. You always seem to know how to make him feel better, Molly."

Molly wasn't so sure, but she needed to talk to her brother anyway. She headed up the creaky old stairs with the banister that looked like a giant snake, and knocked on Marty's door.

"Come in," he said in a muffled voice, as if it was buried in a pillow.

Molly entered and looked around. Marty's room looked exactly the way it had when he was alive, New England Patriots posters on the walls and clothes strewn everywhere. Which was honestly an achievement, as Marty no longer wore clothes.

"Hey," she said, sitting down on the bed. "How's it going?"

"How does it *look*?" snapped Marty.

"Well . . . like an empty room, honestly," said Molly. That got a reluctant chuckle out of him, which she thought was as good an opening as any. "So, Marty. You were always weird, right? But now you are acting *extra* weird. What's going on?"

She could feel Marty sit up on the bed. He hesitated and tried speaking several times.

"Come on, Marty," said Molly. "We can't check the school

until tomorrow, so there's no point stressing now. I get that this is freaky, but it was also still just some lights and a couple of musical instruments. And public humiliation for me, but that's more my problem than yours. Besides, maybe whoever did it was trying to help me? Like I thought you were?"

Marty shook his head. "It's not that. Or maybe it is. I don't know."

"Okaaay . . ." said Molly.

Marty took a deep breath. "Look . . . I hadn't said this before because I wasn't sure it was real, or it was just in my head . . . but then after what happened at the concert . . ." He trailed off, invisible eyes that only Molly could sense staring into the middle distance.

"Marty, you're scaring me," said Molly.

"*I'm* scaring me!" said Marty, looking up at her. "The thing is . . . remember how I had no memory of the explosion? How I just woke up in this bed the next day with no body? But also with straight-up magic powers, which was honestly a nice consolation prize."

Molly nodded. Marty hesitated again before continuing.

"Well . . . it's just that I've started to have . . . *flashes*. Of what happened."

"What?!" said Molly. "Oh no, not of . . ."

"What? Oh, no, not dying," said Marty. "More of just before everything went . . . kabloom."

Molly didn't think that sounded much better. "Okay . . ."

"So, what I think I remember is I went into Mom's art studio to ask her if she'd washed my gray Pats sweatshirt," he continued. "And it makes no sense, but . . . I'm not even sure Mom had the kiln *on* when the explosion happened."

"What do you mean?" said Molly. She could feel Marty looking at her desperately.

"I mean, I definitely don't remember it being hot, or hearing anything rumbling like it was about to blow. Just a sudden big flash of light . . . and then I woke up. In bed, and now a poltergeist."

Molly stood up from the bed and started pacing around the room. "So, you're saying . . ."

"I'm saying that I'm not sure what happened that day was an accident. Not anymore. And if *that* wasn't an accident . . . how do we know whoever did this isn't trying again?"

Molly stopped dead in her tracks. "You mean . . . like throwing a piano? You think that was someone trying to *kill* me?" She gasped. "My violin string did break out of nowhere!"

"Exactly. Molly . . . I think a witch might *actually* have cursed our house. Or maybe someone is trying to finish the job Goody Proxmire started."

"Or both," said Molly. They stared at each other.

As night fell, Molly and Marty took the opportunity to sneak out of the house. Fortunately for them, Timothy was out on a date and their parents were distracted by Dyandra's bedtime story. Dad was turning the pages while Mom read aloud from an old copy of *Peter Rabbit* as the twins crept past Dyandra's bedroom door. "*. . . But don't go into Mr. McGregor's garden,*" said Mom brightly as they passed unnoticed, "*your father had an accident there; he was put in a pie by Mrs. McGregor.*"

"BUNNEH BRAAAAAINS!" squealed Dyandra enthusiastically, her shrieks of delight echoing down the hall. Molly and Marty took the opportunity to head down the stairs as quickly as they could, grateful that the noise their sister made concealed the extra squeaky floorboards.

Finally, they made it out the front door. "I don't even know what you think we'll find," said Molly as they headed toward the ruins that stood near their house. "The fire department and the cops all inspected Mom's studio already."

"I dunno, signs, I guess," said Marty. "Something that fits with what I remember."

Molly shuddered and looked up. The moon was full, and they could hear the calls of seagulls over the Atlantic just a few blocks away.

"I mean, it's a nice night for it," said Marty. Molly frowned at him. "What? If I'm going to investigate the scene of my death, I'm glad it's pretty out!"

"Well, I guess that's one way of looking at it," said Molly. They were in front of Mom's ruined art studio now, a burned-out husk of the old building. Molly had avoided even looking at it for the first six months, and she had definitely never been this close up since the accident. Bits of broken wall stood like jagged teeth in the moonlight. Fragments of metal and ceramic, parts of Mom's art installations, still lay scattered on the floor.

Molly shuddered as they crossed the threshold. Her mom's studio had always creeped her out due to its former role as a crematorium. And that was back when it was bright and colorful and airy, filled ceiling to floor with her mother's work. Now she was very glad Marty was there. Which probably made her one of the few girls in the world grateful to be exploring a derelict crematorium *with* a ghost.

The moon was bright so they didn't need a flashlight, but Molly brought one anyway. She waved it around in no particular direction.

"See anything yet?"

"Not yet," said Marty. "NO, wait! Back to where you were."

Molly turned the light back to the base of what had once been a funeral furnace, and then their mother's ceramics kiln.

Black scorch marks were still visible, but underneath it . . .

"What *is* that?" she said, crouching down to get a closer look. Someone had carved something into the brick. It looked like a flower made up of overlapping circles.

"That's an apotropaic mark." Molly and Marty yelped as they heard an unearthly British voice behind them. They turned to see Mr. Bones, silhouetted against the night sky. "People used to carve them onto houses . . . to ward off witches and other evildoers."

"Oh . . . uh . . . that's interesting?" squeaked Molly.

"I was just taking an evening stroll among the tombstones," said Mr. Bones. "I take it you are in the habit, too?"

"Y-yes?" said Molly.

"It's funny you've found one of those. There was a similar mark on the house where I grew up. Seventeenth century, we believe. I'm surprised to see one here in the New World."

Molly nodded shakily. "Well . . . we had witches, too. Or believed we did."

"Ah yes. Salem. Roehampton. I suppose it makes sense that people imported their protections against witches along with their belief in them." Mr. Bones made a sound like something between a groan and a wheeze. It took Molly a second to realize he was laughing. She giggled nervously back.

"Well, I should be going . . ." she said as she backed toward what remained of the doorway.

"Run as soon as you're out of eyesight!" hissed Marty.

"Did you hear that?" said Mr. Bones.

"NO!" yelped Molly.

Mr. Bones smiled, which somehow was even more frightening than his spooky resting face. "Well, I shan't keep you. By the way, please give my compliments to your housekeeper."

"Uh . . . housekeeper?" Molly paused her escape out of confusion.

"Yes, rather absentminded lady, wears a kaftan? You must know her, I've seen her floating about the place several times. Talking about paints and baked goods? Anyway, please tell her that what I assume must be her cheese rolls are extremely tasty."

"Okay!" said Molly, in a much higher than usual speaking voice.

"Well, I should be off," said Mr. Bones as he retreated into the darkness. "Ta for now." Molly and Marty stared after him, before turning and running back into the house.

"Oh no, no, no, no, no," said Molly once they were safely back in Marty's room. "He can see Mom. He can actually see Mom."

"I mean, it's not the first time someone outside the family has," said Marty. "And most people can *hear* her. Even when she thinks she's whispering."

"Yes, but it's normally only babies, dogs, and that weird old fortune-teller on the pier one time!" said Molly. "Not someone who *literally works with Dad.*"

Marty paused. "You have a point." His eyes suddenly widened. "You know . . . all that stuff at the concert happened right after he showed up. You don't think—"

"I—I don't know. I don't know anything anymore." Molly shook her head. "But we really need to tell Mom and Dad about it. And also that he's sneaking around the cemetery at night."

Marty nodded. "And *I'll* tell them about what I think I can remember. If there really is someone after us, we need to warn them."

Chapter
Seven

It was Monday morning. So far Operation Warn Mom and Dad was not going well.

"Look, I double-checked Mr. Bones's credentials and references before hiring him," said Dad. "He used to work at Highgate Cemetery in London. Then he married an American, came to the States, and worked at Graceland Cemetery in Chicago before moving here—"

"But, Dad—" said Molly, before Dad interrupted her interruption.

"He has no criminal record or anything sketchy," said Dad firmly. "He is just a highly experienced assistant cemetery keeper, nothing more. And if he likes looking at the gravestones, well I can't blame him! They are *fascinating*, especially the older ones."

"Dad, this is not a time to be waxing poetic about Puritan death's head motifs!" said Molly. "We could be in serious danger!"

"Sweetie, while I agree we should be careful, your father and I have been talking," said Mom. "We thought we might need to clue Mr. Bones in anyway."

"What?" screeched Molly and Marty.

"Whhargh!" said Dyandra, pleased that other family members were also making loud noises.

"Well, there was always a chance that he would *hear* your mom, working so close to the house," said Dad. "So we figured it was best to let him know about the Big Secret. We were going to wait a while, but if he can *see* her, too . . ."

"Besides, it might be nice to talk with someone outside the family regularly," added Mom. "I mean, normally it's only babies and animals who can see me."

"Nnnyaah!" said Dyandra.

"Oh, and of course all of my favorite people!" said Mom, almost ruffling Dyandra's head.

"But we don't even know if we can trust him!" said Marty, as all the kitchenware on the table started to vibrate. "What if what I remember is . . ."

He didn't get to finish his sentence as his mother whirled around, her kaftan inflated like a great sail. She looked uncharacteristically furious.

"Look, I refuse to hear any more nonsense about the curse. OR the accident." Her voice suddenly turned very quiet. "We all know whose fault that was."

Molly and Marty looked at each other, suddenly guilty. Until now, they hadn't really ever brought up the topic of what happened. Well, not since that first day, when Mom and Marty realized what had happened. Mom had tried to hug Marty but went straight through him. Then she had sobbed and apologized over and over for the mistakes she'd made when converting the crematorium, and Marty had told her it was okay, since he basically had superpowers now. And that had made them all laugh for the first time since . . . well, dying.

Molly had always assumed since then that her mom was fine and was dealing with death in her own spacey way. She hadn't realized what a sore subject it was for her.

Marty seemed to realize now, too. "I'm sorry, Mom, I didn't mean to—"

"Marty, not now," said Dad softly.

"I just don't want to hear any more about it," said Mom, her voice hollow and final. "And I don't want to hear any more accusations about poor Mr. Bones!"

Timothy entered the kitchen just in time to break the tension. Molly had never been more grateful for his obliviousness.

"Hey, Dad, can I borrow the hearse?" he said, grabbing the keys from the table.

"Ha-ha, I take it your date went well yesterday?" said Dad. Timothy just nodded, shoved a bagel in his mouth, and headed out the door. Molly shook her head in wonder. After the Christmas concert, she was even more confused as to what Kaitlyn saw in her brother.

Molly turned back to her mom, a little nervous that she might still be upset. Fortunately, Mom was already distracted.

"Oh, Jeremy, I've been meaning to ask," she said, almost back to her normal ghostly self. "Does Mr. Bones have anyone to spend Christmas with? We should invite him if he's going to be all alone."

Dad smiled. "I'll talk to him today. I know he moved to Roehampton after getting divorced, so—"

Dad was cut off by the tolling of their doorbell. Molly sighed. It was Grace and Ben, ready to drive her to school.

Time to face the music.

It was somehow even worse than Molly expected. From the moment she entered the gates, the whispers started. They continued all the way through first, second, third, and fourth period—Molly's classmates muttering something to one another, looking quickly at Molly, and then turning away.

It continued through lunch, where even the lunch ladies talked among themselves. Molly could hear words like "traumatized" and "coming up to the anniversary" and "poor kid," and cringed at every one.

The only bright spot in Molly's entire day was that she and Grace were back to being best friends. Seeing everyone whispering about Molly had brought out all of Grace's protective instincts, and she had spent the morning glaring at anyone who attempted to gossip within earshot. And, Molly had to admit, it was a relief to have a big problem she could actually talk to Grace about. Even if that problem was public humiliation and the murmurs of the whole school.

Unfortunately for Molly, last period meant the Roehampton witch trials project and further forced partnership with the dreaded Cara Hartman. And since Grace was partnered with Brayden that meant she was basically doing the project by herself, which left Molly with limited protection. Worse, Cara had been in fine form today, responsible for the loudest whispers and the meanest giggles.

"So, do you think you're up to working today?" said Cara

overly sweetly as the class headed into the library. "I mean, after the concert, I wasn't sure you would show."

"Oh, I'm *fine*," said Molly, gritting her teeth. "Though I am really mad that someone messed with my strings before the concert. I know I'd just changed them."

Cara shrugged. "Maybe you messed up."

"I definitely did not—" hissed Molly. She stopped mid-argument as she saw Ms. Lewis come up to them. Cara smirked.

"Molly, can I have a word?" said Ms. Lewis, her voice soft. Molly nodded and smiled brightly at the suggestion, even as she felt her stomach drop and the pins and needles return to her fingers. She hated the kind of awkward conversations that always followed "Can I have a word?" and she knew exactly what this one would be about. Molly followed Ms. Lewis to the side of the library, shoulders slumped. And as she did, she could see Cara was watching her, eyes narrowed the whole way.

Molly turned back to Ms. Lewis, who was of course giving her *that look*. "Molly," she said gently, "I'm sure this hasn't been a fun day. How are you holding up?"

Molly shrugged as casually as she could. She liked Ms. Lewis and she didn't want her to feel sorry for her. Frustratingly, playing it off as nothing only made Ms. Lewis look at her with even more sympathy.

"I'm okay," said Molly, trying very hard to show how relaxed she was. Ms. Lewis definitely wasn't buying it.

"Okay," she said. "Still, I think that given, uh, *everything*, it would be a good idea to get your dad in to talk. Could you let him know I want to see him?"

Molly didn't think she'd be able to keep the panic out of her voice, so she simply nodded silently. Ms. Lewis smiled. "Don't worry, you're not in trouble. You can come along, too, if you'd like—I just want to check in with you all."

Molly nodded again. The pins and needles were traveling up her neck and ears now, and she was getting increasingly dizzy and light-headed. This was not good. Definitely not good.

But then, to Molly's complete and total relief, the lights above them flickered gently. Everyone looked up, including Ms. Lewis. Marty slipped back into the room during the distraction, the library door opening and closing slowly enough for no one but Molly to notice.

"The auditorium's free, and they have scaffolding to fix the lights that they haven't taken down yet," Marty whispered into her ear. "This is our chance to investigate."

Chapter
Eight

☙

Molly needed no convincing to leave.

"Can I have a bathroom pass?" she asked Ms. Lewis, clutching her stomach dramatically. "It's an, um, *emergency*."

"Sure," said Ms. Lewis. She looked strangely disappointed as she filled out the pass. "Go right ahead. Just make sure you let your dad know I want to see him when you get home. I'm pretty much free after school all this week."

Molly nodded, doing her best to look like she was smiling bravely through her pain, and ran out of the room.

"Do you think she bought that?" said Marty as they sped through the hallway toward the auditorium.

"Not sure," said Molly. "Though if she didn't, I guess she didn't care too much to stop me."

"That's not like her," said Marty, frowning. "Not caring, I mean." They were at the school's front hall now, which led directly into the old, high-ceilinged auditorium. Molly checked that no one was around before she answered as quietly as possible.

"Does that matter? It's not like she's a suspect."

"Or *is* she?!" said Marty dramatically. "Nah, just joking. I once saw her cry over a puppy farm video Mr. Anderson showed her. I don't think she's evil witch material." They were at the auditorium now. "Though do we have any suspects other than Mr. Bones?"

"No, but I was thinking . . ." said Molly. "Maybe we should investigate Cara Hartman, too?"

Marty looked shocked. "What? I know she's a horrible person, but do we think she's *that* bad?"

"Well, think about it," said Molly as they sneaked through the auditorium doors. They were the tall, heavy, double kind, and creaked loudly despite her best efforts to open them gently. "Cara totally had motive to ruin the concert, and she even sounded like she had practiced the solo—like she *knew* what was going to happen! Plus, she was in town last year when the accident happened, unlike Mr. Bones."

"Yeah, but Molly . . ." said Marty, frowning as they tiptoed into the darkened room. "Do we really think Cara's a murderer?"

The only light came from the small windows located up high near the ceiling. They threw strange shapes against the scaffolding that had been left behind, like long shadowy figures marching across the walls. Molly's shadow joined them as she and Marty made their way to the front.

She held up her finger for a second in the semidarkness as she considered Marty's question, before slouching in defeat. "No . . . I guess not."

"Exactly," said Marty as he floated to the ceiling. "Anyway, I'm going to take a closer look at those lights."

"Okay, I'll check out the piano," said Molly, feeling her way warily through the gloom to the stage. She wasn't even halfway there before she heard her brother yelp from above.

"Molly!" he shouted. "You're not going to believe it . . . but there's another of those apotra—uh, aptropic—*anyway* there's another one of those spooky anti-witch marks up here! You know, like the one at Mom's old studio that Mr. Bones told us about!"

"You're kidding," said Molly, craning her neck to see.

"No! Did you bring your phone? If we take a photo . . ."

"We could show Mom and Dad?"

"Exactly!"

Molly put her phone in her pocket and started climbing the scaffolding. "On it!"

"Whoa . . . Molly, there's one carved next to every single light!" said Marty as he rushed about the ceiling. "Literally all of them! I just checked!"

Molly reached the top of the scaffold and tossed him her phone. Invisible hands caught it, and started taking photos immediately, the capture sound effect going off in quick succession.

As her brother stayed busy, Molly walked over to the edge of the scaffold platform. While she was up here, she might as well take a closer look, too. Leaning over the edge of the railing and squinting, she saw that Marty was right. There, drawn next to every light within her line of sight, was a tiny ring of circles, just like the one they found on Mom's old kiln.

Steadying herself with one hand, Molly climbed up on the first rung of the scaffold railing and leaned even farther over. Stretching out as far as she could, she managed to just brush the mark closest to her with her spare hand. Black dust came away on her fingers, almost like the mark had been burned into the ceiling.

"Careful, Moll," said Marty, suddenly hovering nervously next to her.

"I'm being careful!" said Molly as she almost slipped. She scowled at him.

"I'm just saying, you can check the photos once I'm done. No use risking your life." Marty gave an invisible shrug. "Though I guess there's a pretty high chance you'll still stick around even if—"

"Don't. Don't even go there," said Molly. She wobbled as she heard the loud creak of the auditorium doors, followed by the sound of some familiar footsteps. Oh no, not . . .

"Molly?" said Grace as she shuffled in nervously, light streaming in behind her. "Molly, are you in here?"

Just stay quiet, thought Molly as she froze in place, balanced precariously with her hand still outstretched. Pinpricks of panic shot up and down her arms. *And please, please, Grace, don't look up.*

Above Molly's head, the lights started flickering. Grace looked up.

And as she did, Molly felt her support hand slip. The world turned upside down as she tumbled over the edge of the railing. Time seemed to slow as she saw the ground coming toward her, Grace's screams echoing in her ears as she fell. This was it. Molly closed her eyes and braced herself for impact.

Instead, she was temporarily winded by a pair of ghostly hands grabbing her by the knees and armpits. "Gotcha!" said Marty. Molly opened her eyes and saw that she was hovering halfway to the floor.

"Oh my gosh, Marty, thank you!" she gasped. "Seriously, I thought I was—" She trailed off as she saw Grace. Who had stopped screaming and was now staring at Molly, eyes wide with shock and horror. Molly looked down. She was about seven feet off the ground, with no visible sign of support. This was less than good.

"Okay, Grace, I know this must look really, *really* weird," she said. "But I swear I can expl—"

She was cut off by the sound of her friend screaming. Louder and harder than Molly had ever heard Grace scream before.

Chapter Nine

The bell for the end of school rang almost immediately. While this did have the bonus of drowning out Grace, it also meant that soon everyone would be leaving their classrooms just in time to see and hear them. Putting everything into words was going to be hard enough with just Grace, but Molly had no idea how she would be able to explain away levitation to the rest of the school. Pins and needles started in her fingers again. She had to get down and get Grace out of screaming distance as soon as possible.

Marty seemed to have the same idea. Molly got that dip-in-a-roller-coaster feeling as they descended quickly, and then several hard bumps to various tender parts of her body as Marty dumped her unceremoniously on the floor. As Molly lay in a flustered pile, she sensed him rush over to the other side of the auditorium.

"Grace, I know you can't hear me, but I'm really, really sorry," he said. Molly didn't like the sound of this, or the series of muffled squeaks that followed. She picked herself up and looked up gingerly, nervous as to what she would see.

Grace had finally, thankfully, stopped screaming. However, and less thankfully, this was because Marty had one invisible hand clamped over her mouth. Molly winced.

"It's okay, Grace, it's just Marty!"

"MMMPH?!" said Grace through Marty's ghost hand. She did not seem comforted at all by Molly's words. Molly silently cursed herself and tried again.

"I'm so sorry, I know this must seem, uh . . ." Molly tried to think of a word that adequately covered seeing a friend floating in midair, then getting silenced by the phantom hand of that friend's dead brother. She failed. "Um . . . anyway, I can explain, I swear! Just . . . not here."

"Can I let go now?" said Marty. "This feels weird."

"I bet it feels weirder for her," said Molly. Grace's eyes bugged in confusion behind her now very askew glasses. "Sorry, Grace, that was to Marty. He wants to let go, but um . . .

could you promise not to scream? We really need to make sure we don't draw attention."

"Mmph . . ." Grace nodded as much as she could with a poltergeist restraining her. Her eyes were still bugging out. Marty let go.

Once freed, Grace staggered slightly and opened and closed her mouth several times before any sound came out. "Wh-what is *happening?*" she finally spluttered. Molly ran over to her and put her arm around her.

"I'll explain everything, once we're away from the school," she said as she led Grace out of the auditorium, doors still squeaking loudly. "But first we need to go. *Now.*"

The auditorium led directly into the front hall and main exit. Molly sighed in almost relief. It was still empty . . . for now. Molly could hear students' voices echoing down the hallways, happy for the end of the day. Any moment they would be rushing through, making their escape with an increasingly floppy Grace that much harder.

"What were you doing in *there?*" said a familiar, snotty voice behind them. Molly suppressed a yelp. Turning slowly, her stomach dropped as she saw Cara hovering in the corner like a very neatly dressed shadow. "Weren't you supposed to be in the library? Working on *our* project?" she said, eyes narrowed.

"I *was*," said Molly as she tried to prop up Grace, who

was now as limp as a noodle and smiling vaguely into space. "And then the bell rang, and I had to pick up some stuff I left during the Christmas concert. Class is *over*, you know."

Cara raised one eyebrow and looked from Molly to Grace. Molly smiled blandly, and tried to ignore the prickling sensation at the back of her neck. Next to her, Grace giggled at nothing and nodded.

"I think we might have broken Grace," whispered Marty into her ear. Molly studiously ignored him and heaved Grace around to face the main exit. The door to the left of her opened, and students started to stream out. She tried to pick up her pace, almost dragging Grace in the process. Invisibly, Marty took her other arm.

"Grace and I are going home now," she called over her shoulder to Cara. "So, bye!"

As they pulled Grace in a wobbly, zigzag route out of the school, Molly didn't dare look back again. But she knew, she just knew, that Cara was staring at them the entire way out.

About an hour later, Molly and Grace were sitting on a stone wall by the beach by themselves. Marty had headed home without them, telling Molly pointedly, "You guys probably have a lot to talk about. You should be honest for a change."

It was a beautiful late afternoon. For a supposedly haunted and cursed town, Roehampton looked especially like a picture postcard today. The waves lapped gently at the shore, and a small gray seal sat sunning itself on some nearby rocks. The winter sun cast faint late afternoon light across the bay and the tall white lighthouse that overlooked it all. It seemed to make everything Molly said sound that much weirder in comparison.

Rubbing her hands nervously across the uneven wall, Molly tried to steady herself. She glanced at her friend. Grace had taken Molly's tale of death, resurrection, and potential murder surprisingly well, all things considered. She hadn't even screamed again. Admittedly, Molly had almost finished explaining everything to her, and in that time Grace had said literally nothing, but that still counted as not screaming. Instead she had just stared at Molly, her eyes two stunned O's.

Molly swallowed again and continued. "Uh, yeah, so then we found Dyandra in the graveyard later that day. She was one of our most recent burials and had managed to chew her way out of her coffin. We found her by her groans. And, um, since neither of her parents rose from the dead with her— they'd all died at the same time in a car crash—we thought we'd better take her in."

Grace still hadn't reacted any further, except that her left eye had started to twitch. Molly tried to ignore that.

"Um, we did check to see if she had any living relatives, obviously. And we thought about calling CPS, too. But then we were, like, are they even the right people if she's legally dead? And also technically speaking, dead?" said Molly, desperately scanning Grace's face. "But um, yeah. That's pretty much all of it."

Silence descended on the beach. Grace didn't move except to blink a few times, as if trying to focus. A tiny frown crept between her eyebrows.

"Grace?" said Molly, wondering whether she needed to shake her. Grace finally closed her eyes and took a deep, agonizingly slow breath. The air around them cooled as the sun ducked behind a cloud, as if to hide from what was to come.

"So . . . the reason you've been acting like . . . *well* . . . all year . . ." said Grace, opening her eyes but not looking at Molly, "is because . . ."

"Right," said Molly. "I'm so, *so* sorry, Grace. I didn't know how to tell you. I mean I tried to, a few times. But then I chickened out. I don't know why. And we needed to make sure that we kept everything secret. Like I said."

"So . . . you didn't think you could trust me?" said Grace in a tiny voice, now fixated on her feet.

"Well . . . no," said Molly. "I mean, that is *no*, I know you would never tell anyone, honestly."

"Then didn't your parents trust me?"

"Oh no!" said Molly. "They've even been telling me to tell you."

"Then what was the problem?" said Grace, finally turning to face Molly again. Her lips were pressed very tightly together, which was probably not a good sign. Molly felt her stomach drop.

"I . . ." Molly paused before finding her words. Consequences or not, she was tired of lying to Grace. "I guess . . . I thought it would be weird. That you would think *I* was weird." Molly pulled her scarf in tighter against the sudden wind now blowing down the beach. "That you would treat me differently, that you wouldn't want to hang out as much if I came with ghosts."

"Okay . . ." said Grace. She stood up, her hair blowing wildly. Two red spots were beginning to form on her cheeks. Molly gulped. She had never seen Grace look this mad. Not even that one time Brayden had suggested Mary Shelley's books were really written by her husband.

"Grace, I—"

"So you're telling me that I've spent the past year thinking you are mad at me, and that I did or said something wrong, and that you don't like me anymore *because you decided I would reject you*? Without checking with me first?" Grace's nostrils were flaring now. Molly shrank back instinctively.

"Well, when you put it like that . . ."

"I can't BELIEVE you think I would do that!" yelled Grace. "I get that you would want to protect your family, and I would understand if this was just to keep you all safe! But if this is just about you thinking I wouldn't like you because your family is different, then I—I . . ." Grace shook her head and flung her arms open. "Do you think I would *ever* stop hanging out with someone over something like that?"

"No," said Molly into her scarf, her voice getting wobbly. The tears were coming again, and she couldn't stop them. "No, you would never do that. . . . But I thought you might put up with m-me even though you didn't want to. Just because you are n-nice."

Grace stood and stared at her for a moment. Molly cringed and waited for what felt like an eternity. She understood if Grace didn't want to be her friend anymore, and Molly felt waves of shame and regret flood through her body. She didn't mean to ruin everything, but it kept on happening. She was so stupid.

But then Grace sighed. Pulling Molly up to standing, she gave her a bear hug almost as all-enveloping as her dad's. Molly hugged her back with relief.

"Listen, you *idiot*," said Grace, "I don't care if you are weird, or your family is weird. They were honestly like that before the accident—that's why I like them. That's why I like *you*."

Molly rubbed her nose and sniffed. "R-really?"

"Really," said Grace firmly. "If I wanted to be friends with someone boring, I would hang out with Cara Hartman or something."

Above them the winter sun broke through the clouds, and even the little gray seal on the rocks seemed to bark in approval. "Oh, Grace," said Molly, feeling better than she had in months, but still sobbing. "Y-you are the best friend ever. I am so, *so* sorry. I don't deserve you."

"Oh, shut up," said Grace. "I love you, you goof. You're my best friend, too." She pulled out of their hug, and held Molly by her shoulders. "Just don't ever assume I won't love you for you *ever* again. Understand?"

Molly nodded shakily. "I won't, I promise."

Grace smiled and linked arms with her. "Good."

The girls huddled against the winter cold as they walked down the beach, in the first comfortable silence between them in almost a year. Molly smiled to herself, feeling lighter and not minding the earache she was getting from the wind. She and Grace were back to being best friends. Real best friends. Perhaps things would work out after all.

Chapter
Ten

"This is never going to work out," said Marty.

It was the following day after school, and Grace, Molly, and Marty were gathered in Molly's room to work out their next steps. After Grace had been filled in about the potential curse and attempts on the Dades' lives, she volunteered to do anything she could to help out. Molly accepted gratefully, equally glad that she and Grace were back to normal and that someone else believed her and her brother.

"Stop," she said to Marty as she looked carefully over her shoulder. Mom had been so thrilled to speak with someone outside the family again, that she had been dipping in and out of the room constantly since Grace had arrived to make random conversation. So far they had talked about the weather, Grace's dads, the best way of proofing bread, and whether plants had souls. All of this made Molly's attempts to secretly investigate Mr. Bones behind her mother's back significantly more difficult. "It's a solid plan."

"What, you think if we just follow Mr. Bones around we'll catch him doing some evil plotting or something?" said Marty. "Maybe some casual murder?"

"What's Marty saying?" said Grace.

"Nothing important," said Molly, glaring in Marty's direction. Grace's phone beeped.

"Marty says that's a lie," said Grace, reading from the message on her phone. "He says that this has no chance of working, and following Mr. Bones around town is not a plan, it's stalking."

Marty smirked.

"Do *you* have any better ideas, *Marty*?" snapped Molly. She was not enjoying her brother's new way of communicating with her best friend. Marty raised an invisible finger for a moment as if considering, then slumped in his seat.

"Well . . . no."

"He says no," said Grace, still reading from her phone.

"I know." Molly sighed. "And seeing as you don't have

anything helpful to suggest, Marty, we are doing my idea."

"Still stalking," said Marty.

Grace's phone beeped. "Um, do you *want* me to read this to you?" she said to Molly.

"Probably not," said Molly as she peered out her bedroom window at the cemetery keeper's lodge. It stood kitty-corner to the Dades' house, a small, solid-brick building built in the 1950s with the hope it would be more fireproof than the previous ones. As it had already survived getting hit by lightning twice so far, it was doing very well. "Anyway, we need to hustle. Mr. Bones should be finishing up right around now."

As if on cue, the cemetery keeper's lodge door opened, and a thin, black-clad figure emerged. "Speak of the devil . . ." said Molly. Grace and Marty joined her at the window, and together they watched Mr. Bones stalk across the graveyard.

"Ooh, Mr. Bones is walking home super evilly," said Marty in Molly's ear. "That's totally enough to convince Mom and Dad."

"Shut up."

"What did he say now?" said Grace. Her phone beeped again. "Oh, thanks!"

Molly rolled her eyes as she heard Grace chuckle guiltily at Marty's message and was about to retort when something caught her eye. Mr. Bones had stopped, as if frozen in place for a few moments. Then he made a sudden detour in the opposite direction of the main gates, moving much faster than he had before. From this distance he looked like a large black beetle scampering across a toy cemetery.

He scuttled purposefully to a tombstone and crouched down. It was hard to tell from this far away, but it looked like he had his hands in the grave dirt and was . . . digging? She could make out his pale hands scrabbling almost frantically in the earth. Next to her, Marty and Grace had gone quiet. They had seen him, too.

"So yes, Marty," said Molly as she zoomed in with her phone and took a picture. "Mr. Bones is digging up a grave with his bare hands while on his way out. I think that counts as 'walking home evilly.'"

"Okay, granted. But maybe . . ." said Marty. "Actually, no, you're right, this is sketchy."

"Should we follow him?" said Grace, twisting her hands together. She looked like she hoped the answer was no.

"We've got to," said Molly, surprised that she also, deep down, wanted to stay back. It was one thing when Mr. Bones being dangerous was a vague possibility. It was another when it looked like he might really be in the business of enacting curses. She repressed a shudder and squared her shoulders. "If he is trying to hurt us, we need to stop him."

It didn't take long for Molly, Marty, and Grace to speed

down the stairs, through the hallways, past the kitchen, and out the back door into the cemetery. They even managed to avoid Mom trying to start a conversation about scones. Even so, by the time they got there, Mr. Bones was already on the move.

"I'll trail him," said Marty.

"Good call. We'll check out the grave before anyone else disturbs it and catch up once we're done," said Molly, trying not to sound relieved. "We can try to follow Mr. Bones at a distance and take photos."

"A *long* distance," said Grace.

As Marty took off, Molly and Grace shuffled nervously to the grave. Molly could tell it was one of the older ones just from the look of it.

Carved at the top was a disembodied head with wings sprouting on either side. Molly had heard her father give the cemetery tour to tourists hundreds of times and knew that this represented a soul leaving their mortal remains behind and soaring into heaven. She also thought the residents of eighteenth-century Roehampton could have made their soul-leaving-faces less creepy looking. This one's eyes seemed to have sideways pupils, almost like a goat, and they stared at Molly like they knew something about her that she wouldn't like.

"That's a really . . . *intense* inscription," said Grace. Molly peered in closer. Grace was not wrong.

JOSIAH

Son of Zebulon Moffit
and Comfort, his wife

Born 1776
Drowned 1797

Remember me as you pass by,
As you are now, so once was I.
And as I am, so you must be,
Prepare for death and follow me.

"Yeah, they didn't mess around back in those days," said Molly, shivering. She crouched down and cautiously touched the newly disturbed dirt. It looked like a small hole had been dug up and filled back in, all concentrated in a small section next to the headstone.

"Do you think he . . . left something in there?" said Grace, crouching down, too. Her eyes widened suddenly. "Or *took* something?"

"I guess . . . we could check?" said Molly. The two girls looked at each other. Neither seemed to want to plunge handsfirst into grave dirt.

Molly shook her head and sighed, knowing what she had to do. It was *her* house that was cursed, after all. She braced herself. Her dad did similar stuff all the time as part of his job—how hard could it be?

The earth was damp and cold to touch, and moved away easily. Molly worked slowly and carefully, afraid of what she might see.

"Did you find anything?" said Grace, hovering behind her shoulder.

"Not yet . . . *wait*." There was something cool, hard, and flat that Molly's hand could not budge. Frightened, but now intrigued, she dug deeper. Could it be . . . ? "Oh. Right, no." Deflated, Molly slumped back on the ground. "That's just the bottom of the headstone."

"Hey, Grace! Grace's friend! What are you doing there?" said a voice behind them. Molly and Grace yelped and scrambled to their feet.

It was the cool brother and sister tourists who were staying at Grace's dads' place. They approached with several pieces of complicated electronic equipment, looking at Molly and Grace with partly entertained, partly alarmed expressions. Which, Molly mused, made sense seeing as they had caught a couple of middle school kids digging up a grave in broad daylight. Molly glanced down at her hands, still caked in grave dirt, and tried to surreptitiously rub them off on her jeans. This just left streaks of grave dirt down them, so she quickly hid her hands behind her back.

"We . . . uh . . ." she said, trying desperately to think of a reasonable explanation for potentially desecrating someone's mortal remains. "We were helping out my dad with conservation efforts." She glanced over her shoulder at the now exposed hole by Josiah Moffit's grave. "Um, like . . . stabilizing the headstones?"

"Well, good for you!" said the man. "We met earlier, at Grace's dads' B-and-B? I'm Ethan."

"I'm Dee," said the woman. "You're the skeptic kid who lives in the haunted house, right?"

"Right. I'm Molly, and you're the brother and sister who like ghost hunting," said Molly, pleased to be remembered and hoping to steer the conversation away from grave digging. "Have you guys seen anything spooky yet?"

Ethan and Dee grinned at each other. "A couple of things," said Dee. "We got some ghost orbs on camera at the museum and what sounds like a spectral voice at the college! Though I guess you think those are probably technical problems with the camera and raccoons or something."

Molly forced herself to laugh. It came out slightly squeaky. "Right."

"We're going to devote a whole episode of our paranormal podcast to what we've found at Roehampton," continued Dee.

"It's called *Myth and Westons*," said Ethan. "You should look it up."

"Oh, awesome," said Molly.

"We're actually recording stuff for it right now—you can't get better than a cursed *and* haunted cemetery," said Dee. "Our listeners are going to love it!"

"Hey, would you and/or your dad be up for doing an interview?" said Ethan. "I think getting a skeptic to describe their experiences would be a really interesting angle."

"Ooh, we could do it inside the house and then conclude with a ghost hunt!" said Dee. "I bet our listeners would really love exclusive footage of a cursed and haunted cemetery keeper's *house*."

"I bet we'd find some great stuff!" said Ethan. "Has anyone done a paranormal investigation on your property before?"

Molly thought of all that complicated equipment pointed directly at her spacey mom, who could be heard even without technological assistance. She blanched, trying to think of an excuse. "Um . . . I guess I could ask my dad. But um . . . he's been kinda weird since Mom died." Molly told herself that this was technically not a lie, because her dad was indeed still weird; he had just *always* been weird. The Westons didn't need to know that.

Molly braced herself for *that look*. Instead, to her surprise and relief, Ethan and Dee smiled at her ruefully. Like they were all part of the same messed-up club. "Sure," said Dee as Ethan nodded. "We know how *that* goes." Molly felt strangely reassured by this, even if she didn't know what to say next. As she rubbed her arm in awkward silence, accidentally smearing grave dirt on her coat, Grace came to her rescue.

"Hey, actually, we're doing a school project on the Roehampton witches," she said. "Have you covered anything about old-timey witchcraft on your podcast?" Grace glanced at Molly. "Specifically curses?"

"Oh, definitely!" said Dee, looking surprised but pleased.

"Episode twenty-eight, 'By the Pricking of My Thumbs,' is a good one for that stuff," added Ethan.

"Cool! Do you remember any signs of being cursed?" said Grace. "You know, for research purposes."

"Well, I guess first off," said Dee, stroking her chin, "there have been reports of pricking sensations all over the body . . ."

"Hence the episode title," said Ethan.

Molly felt the familiar pins and needles return to her hands. Pins and needles . . . *also known as pricking sensations!* Her head began to spin, and she felt like every breath she took only got in half the air she needed.

"Also dizziness, shortness of breath," continued Dee. "Nausea, stomach complaints. Just generally not feeling great."

"I see," squeaked Molly as her stomach twisted into knots. Grace looked at her nervously, sensing something was wrong.

"And then it could progress to boils, hallucinations, loss of limbs, even death!" said Dee, who seemed too enthused to notice. "So yeah, you should be really careful when upsetting a witch. If you believe in them, that is."

Molly started laughing nervously again. "Right! Right. Good thing I don't!"

"You should check out the podcast," said Ethan with a hopeful grin. "It's got a lot of history and lore that'll be interesting, even for skeptics like yourself."

"We definitely will!" said Grace as she gently led Molly away. "Thanks for the witchcraft information!"

"Good luck with your project," said Dee. "Watch out for those raccoons!"

Chapter
Eleven

It took Molly and Grace a while to find Marty—he couldn't send messages when he wasn't near a phone, and he had no way of receiving them. When they finally tracked him down, he was watching Mr. Bones peer closely at the rambling old hawthorn tree just outside the cemetery walls. The exact same old hawthorn tree where Goody Proxmire was buried.

Molly and Grace looked at each other, neither daring to speak. What was Mr. Bones doing? Silently, Molly got her phone out and started filming.

They both yelped loudly as they heard Grace's phone

beep. "Guys, we're supposed to be stealthy here. Why aren't you on silent mode?" Marty suddenly hissed in Molly's ear. The two girls stood still, not daring to move. Mr. Bones briefly looked around, his face still as blank as ever, before turning back to the tree. Molly, Grace, and even Marty, despite his lack of lungs, let out a sigh of relief.

As Grace checked Marty's message, Molly heard him whisper quietly in her ear, "So anyway, after he left the cemetery, he drove to the garden center. I lost him in the crowd getting last-minute Christmas trees, but he came out with a bag of dirt and something in a large brown bottle. I couldn't see the label. Then, instead of driving straight back, he came here. He's been standing at this tree for five minutes. Just staring and taking notes."

Molly's mind reeled. First grave dirt, then buying some *more* dirt? And what was in the bottle? What was Mr. Bones's game? What did this have to do with the tree and the curse?

"Quick, he's moving again!" hissed Marty into her ear. Molly tapped Grace's shoulder, gesturing silently. Grace nodded, and together they trailed Mr. Bones as closely as they dared. Marty swooped ahead of them, hovering right behind Mr. Bones as he stopped at a small black car. The girls crept up closer, trying not to catch Mr. Bones's eye as he opened the car door.

"Good evening," said Mr. Bones, suddenly looking up directly at them, the terrifying smile back on his face as he waved. His black eyes bored into them, as if he could see into their very souls. Molly and Grace clutched each other with one arm, and waved back with their free hands.

"Good evening!" they said, smiling stiffly and failing to sound casual. They jumped again as their phones started beeping frantically at the exact same time. Grateful for the distraction, they pulled them out immediately, walking past Mr. Bones as fast as they could.

It was a message from Marty:

I'm getting into his car.

Meet me at Ray's.

Molly, let Mom and Dad know we won't be home for dinner.

Well, you won't be. I don't eat, lol.

Also, silent mode!!!

Marty had been gone long enough for Grace and Molly to have almost finished the cheese fries they were sharing at Ray's Lobster Shack and Diner. They barely noticed, huddled into the red vinyl booth, deep in conspiratorial conversation.

"So, what I'm saying is, maybe we didn't find anything because he *took* something from the grave," said Molly, keeping her voice low. "Like maybe a bone, or just a sample of grave dirt. That uh, he's going to mix with the soil he just bought from the garden center."

"Or maybe," said Grace, leaning in closer and looking over her glasses meaningfully. "Mr. Bones is a *vampire*."

Molly burst out laughing. Grace scowled.

"Seeing who your mom, brother, *and* sister are, are you really going to write off vampires?" she said.

"Fair point," conceded Molly. "But what makes you think vampires specifically?"

A shadow fell across the table. The girls started and looked up.

"Anything else?" It was the teenage server. She wore a lot of eyeliner, a pair of jolly red antlers, and an annoyed expression. Molly bit her lip and counted the coins and singles she and Grace had cobbled together on the table.

"We're good, thanks."

The server scowled even harder, if possible, and stalked off to the other side of the restaurant, antlers bouncing as she went.

"So you were saying," said Molly once the server was no longer in earshot. "Vampires."

"Okay, so I've read *Dracula*," said Grace. "And he needed the earth he was buried in to sleep."

"But then why steal someone else's grave dirt?" said Molly. "Oh, unless maybe something happened to his own! Like it was lost somehow?"

Grace nodded enthusiastically. "And then maybe he couldn't take too much without being noticed, so then he needed to mix it in with some more earth. Which is why he bought the potting soil!"

"But what about the brown bottle?" said Molly. "What was that for?"

Grace frowned. "Embalming fluid, maybe?"

"But you can't get that from a garden center," said Molly. "And do vampires need to embalm themselves?"

"Hmm, well then maybe it *is* for a spell," said Grace. She gasped. "Maybe it's for the curse—"

"Hey, Molly, hey, Grace!" Molly turned to see Timothy, who had just entered Ray's with Kaitlyn on his arm and a big, goofy grin on his face. "Kaitlyn, you met my little sister and her friend Grace yet?"

"No, but I, uh, saw Molly at her concert. How's it going?" Kaitlyn smiled at Molly sympathetically, which made Molly bristle. She did not want Kaitlyn's sympathy. She wanted Kaitlyn to think she was awesome.

Molly sat up straighter as if she was not bothered at all by her recent public humiliation. "Oh, yeah, fine thanks," she said. "I honestly think I was sabotaged or something."

"Yeah, Molly and Mart— uh, I mean *just Molly* thinks someone's cursed our house," said Timothy. "For real."

"Shut up, Timothy," said Molly, willing him to go away.

"What's wrong? You were talking about it earlier today. And *all* yesterday."

"Shut *up*."

"You were!" said Timothy, annoyingly confused. "You were, like, 'We're really cursed and they were trying to kill me at the Christmas concert!' and I was, like, 'Who's they?' and Dad was, like, 'I don't think death-by-exploded-lightbulb is possible, Moll.' Remember? It was only yesterday."

"Aww, leave them alone," chided Kaitlyn, so sweet and lovely that Molly suspected cute woodland animals had helped her get dressed that morning. "I used to like making up fun mysteries when I was a kid, too." Molly sulked in her seat even harder.

"Oh yeah, Molly totally does that," said Timothy, like he had just realized something interesting. "Like right now she thinks our dad's new assistant is in league with Goody Proxmire. Even though Goody Proxmire died, like, a *hundred* years ago!"

"Three hundred and fifty," said Molly. "There are *literally* signs for the anniversary everywhere."

"Tim, don't be mean," said Kaitlyn.

"I'm just describing!" said Timothy, smiling as he

ruffled Molly's hair affectionately. "Molly doesn't mind, do you, Moll?"

"I hate you so much right now," said Molly.

"See!" said Timothy, beaming. "Aww, I hate you, too, sis!"

"Well, anyway," said Kaitlyn, who looked amused, "we should pick up our order. The guys are waiting for us." She shot another sympathetic smile to Molly and led Timothy to the front counter. "Nice meeting you properly, Molly, and you too, Grace."

"See you back home, Moll!" Timothy waved enthusiastically over his shoulder. "Bye, Grace!"

As he waved without looking, Timothy accidentally knocked into the server with the eyeliner and antlers. She stumbled and nearly dropped clam chowder on Mr. Anderson, who was eating dinner dolefully by himself in a corner booth. "Whoa, didn't see you there, Em!" Timothy said as he steadied the server. "Sorry about that."

"It's okay!" said the server, no longer scowling through her eyeliner, but blushing as she tried to balance her tray. "No damage done."

"Okay, cool." Timothy nodded. "Nice antlers."

The guy behind the counter called Timothy's name. Tim turned to him and grabbed his order. "Hey, thanks buddy." He grinned. The guy smiled and looked down before quickly getting back to his work.

Meanwhile the server with the antlers was still staring after Timothy and Kaitlyn. She whispered something that sounded suspiciously like *"He knows my name!"* under her breath.

Molly turned to Grace, hoping to find someone who hadn't lost their mind. "Ugh, he is *so* annoying," she said, rolling her eyes. "Right, Grace? *Grace?*"

But Grace was also staring dreamily at the exit. "Sorry, what?"

"Never mind." Molly sighed. "So we were talking about Mr. Bones—" She stopped short as she noticed the door to the diner slowly open and shut, by a force invisible to most people.

"Okay, wait, Marty's back!"

Chapter Twelve

Molly shuffled along in her seat to make room and felt her brother sit down next to her. Grace's eyes widened. She was almost looking in the right place.

"Ugh!" said Marty.

"What happened?" said Molly and Grace. Grace's phone beeped several times.

"So," said Marty, "I sneaked into Mr. Bones's apartment after him."

"And?" said Molly, making sure her eyes stayed focused on Grace, who was busy reading her phone. She didn't want the whole *town* to think of her as a staring-into-space-muttering girl.

"And he—" Marty was cut off suddenly by the server with the antlers bringing a large chocolate milkshake to their table.

"Hey, so you're Timothy Dade's sister, right?" she said. Molly nodded. "Well, I know him from school. Anyway, we accidentally made the wrong flavor shake for a customer and this was sent back."

"Okay," said Molly, bewildered, but hoping to end this quickly so that she could keep talking to Marty.

"And I thought, why waste it when I can give it to my friend's sister and her friend?" said the server as she placed down the shake. "So yeah, this is on the house."

"Oh, uh, thanks!" said Molly, still confused. Grace started drinking the milkshake immediately and shrugged at Molly. The server was still hanging around for some reason. "Your brother doesn't uh . . . mention me at all, does he?" she said after an awkward silence. "My name's Emma."

Molly racked her brains. "Emma, who threw that big party a while back?"

"That's Emma Doyle," said the server.

"Um . . . Emma who's on the cheerleading team?" said Molly.

"That's Emma Shapiro." The server scowled and sighed. "Anyway, it doesn't matter. Enjoy."

Molly watched as Emma Not-Doyle-or-Shapiro's antlers

bounced sadly away to a safe distance before turning back to the table.

"You were saying, Marty?" she said, keeping her eyes still trained on Grace.

"So, Mr. Bones is . . . really boring," said Marty. "Like *really* boring. He just did some laundry, made dinner, and watched some British shows on his laptop."

"What?" said Molly.

"I know," said Grace, who had finished reading Marty's messages a while ago. "I was disappointed, too."

"But what about the soil?" said Molly. "And that large bottle he bought?"

"He used that . . . to care for a potted plant," said Marty.

"Okay," said Molly. "But are you sure it wasn't an *evil* plant? Like something poisonous, or for a spell, or that, like, eats insects or something?"

"No, I don't think so," said Marty. "I'm pretty sure it was a peace lily."

"Ugh!" said Molly, taking a sip of milkshake in frustration. "Oh wow, this is *really* good."

After Molly and Grace finished the really good milkshake, they headed out with Marty. The sky was already nighttime dark, the stars bright, and the air cold. Ray's Lobster Shack and Diner, like most of Roehampton, looked adorable in the day and terrifying at night. In this light the weathered gray shingles looked like the scales of some ancient sea creature, peeled off and slapped on the side of a place that served cheeseburgers and lobster rolls.

Molly pulled her scarf in tighter, her breath hanging in the air. "So . . . what do we have on Mr. Bones now? Some photos?"

"Not enough to convince Mom and Dad," said Marty. "Today was kind of a bust."

"But it still seems like he's up to something," said Molly. "What about the grave? And the tree?" She felt the pins and needles return to her hands. They terrified her now in a way they hadn't before.

"And we don't have any other suspects," said Grace. She stopped and frowned at Molly. "Hey, Molly, are you okay?"

"Yeah, you sorta look like you're in pain," said Marty. "Or have gas."

"I'm fine—" Molly was about to say, but stopped herself. She didn't want to keep secrets anymore. Even if telling the truth made her worries seem more frighteningly real. "Actually, I'm not. I think . . . uh . . . I mean, I don't actually know if this is in my head or not. . . . But it *feels* like it's real. And um . . ."

Molly swallowed as she watched Grace and Marty waiting patiently for her to get to the point. She took a deep breath. "So I think *I* might be cursed. Me specifically, not just the house."

"What?!" said Grace, eyes wide.

"You serious, Moll?" added Marty, his eyes equally wide. Molly nodded and fiddled with the sleeves of her jacket.

"So I've been feeling these pricking sensations in my hands and legs, and I keep on getting dizzy, and out of breath. And I thought it was just stress or lack of exercise or something, but after talking to Dee and Ethan in the cemetery . . ."

"Everything they said about signs you have been cursed match your symptoms!" finished Grace for her. "Oh, Molly, how long has this been going on for?"

"I dunno, a while?" said Molly. "Somewhere around the time of the accident, maybe a little before?"

"Whoa. That fits with the explosion being part of the curse," said Marty. Grace's phone beeped and she gasped as she read Marty's message.

"That makes horrible sense," Grace said. "I mean, I believed you guys before, but now I *really* believe you."

Molly nodded shakily as Grace's phone beeped again.

"I told her that we need to step up our investigation," said Marty. "And expand our range of suspects. Mr. Bones does seem sketchy, but we don't want to miss anything."

"Marty's right," said Grace as she read his message. "I say we try again tomorrow, and keep our eyes peeled for *anything* out of the ordinary. If you've been cursed, then this is way more urgent than we thought."

Molly nodded and tried to ignore the pins and needles now racing up and down her arms and legs. What else could they do?

Grace, as if somehow understanding what Molly needed, hugged her. Then Marty hugged them both. Grace giggled.

"Sorry, Marty, but this feels really weird," said Grace. Her phone beeped, but she didn't break the hug.

Molly smiled despite herself, the pins and needles subsiding just a little. Even if she was cursed, it was good to know she wasn't alone.

Chapter Thirteen

Molly had trouble sleeping that night. Alone with her thoughts, the idea that she and her family were truly cursed felt just a bit more, horribly, real. Tossing and turning, she watched the dim light from her window slowly crawl across the ceiling. This wasn't working. She needed to stretch her legs.

Squinting, she pulled back the curtain. In the pale moonlight, she saw the grave Mr. Bones had been digging. The hole that she and Grace had covered up so carefully earlier that day was now uncovered—and then some.

It now was wide and long enough to hold a body.

Molly gasped, grabbed her phone, and fumbled in the dark for her robe. She needed to take a photo of this before anyone tried to cover it up. Creeping out of her room and down the stairs as quietly as she could, Molly winced at every creaky floorboard. As this was the Dades' house, this was most of them.

Still, miraculously, she made it to the coatrack without waking anyone. Wondering for a moment if she should turn back and fetch Marty, Molly decided against it. She didn't want to go over the loudest landing in New England a second time and risk waking her family.

Instead, she pulled on her jacket over her robe and shoved her feet into her winter boots. Gently opening the back door, she slipped out of the house and used her phone to light her way to the grave.

Once there, Molly immediately regretted her decision. It was not a trick of the light. The hole was definitely real, longer and wider than she had thought, and impossibly deep. Molly stared into it, and it seemed almost bottomless.

She needed to get out of here. Lifting her phone, Molly tried to take a photo with trembling hands, but they were shaking too much to focus. "Come on, come on," she muttered to herself, before suddenly dropping her phone with a start.

An unknown pair of hands were on her back.

"Hello?" said Molly, pins and needles racing up and down her spine. She could feel the breath of whoever this was on the back of her neck, wheezing and labored. She didn't dare turn around. "Hello? Who is this?"

There was no answer. Molly tried to run, but she felt frozen to the spot by something beyond her.

Then the hands pushed her. Forcefully enough to send Molly tumbling over into the open grave. Her feet scrambled, desperately trying to find her footing.

It was too late. Molly fell, screaming, into the endless darkness.

Molly awoke with a start. It may have just been a dream, but the dizziness and the pins and needles were back. "This isn't happening, this isn't happening," she said as she buried her face back into the pillow. Instead, the pricking sensation spread up and down her back and her stomach started doing loops. "No, no, no, no, no," said Molly desperately, the tingling reaching her ears and face now.

She sat up again. Maybe she needed some water. And light. Definitely all the lights needed to be on.

Bleary-eyed, Molly fumbled around her nightstand before locating the lamp and turning it on by shape and memory. The light crackled and buzzed a few times. Then suddenly, it exploded, shattering the glass in the bulb across the nightstand.

Molly screamed and ran from the room.

It took all the Dades ten minutes to calm Molly down enough to explain what happened. "I've been getting pins and needles, like pricking sensations, and my stomach's been feeling weird! That's what happens when a witch curses you!!"

"Who told you it was witchcraft?" said Dad, frowning.

"Um . . . I just heard it," said Molly, looking away. "On a spooky podcast."

"Maybe you should lay off those for a while," said Dad gently. "Though I have to admit, you don't look good." He felt her forehead. "You don't have a fever. But I can run you over to the urgent care clinic?"

Molly shook her head. She didn't think they would be able to cover curses.

"You sure?" said Dad.

"Take the day off at least, sweetie." said Mom "You do really look sick, and with those symptoms . . ."

"Symptoms that I've been cursed by a witch!" said Molly.

"Yeah, but they're also symptoms of, like, stress, and stomach flu, and a whole bunch of other stuff," said Timothy.

"Exploding lightbulbs aren't!" said Molly. "This is the

first time this has happened *inside our house!* What if it means that *they're here!*"

"I think that's probably faulty wiring, pumpkin. We really do need to get the electrics fixed," said Dad.

"Nnnnghh!" said Molly.

"Nnyaaargh!!" said Dyandra enthusiastically. Timothy high-fived her.

"We just need to be realistic here. Witches aren't real, sweetie," said Mom.

"Well, seeing as zombies, ghosts, and poltergeists are definitely real, who's to say witches aren't?" said Molly. "Marty! Say you're with me here!"

"Oh, I'm with you. It's just that I don't get much of a say in any of this," said Marty. "But, yes, Dad, Mom, Timothy, we are totally cursed. I mean LOOK AT US." He lifted a chair into the air for emphasis.

"Marty, put that down right now!" said Mom as Dyandra climbed on the table and tried swiping at it. "And— *Dyandra Nash Dade*!"

"Okay, I think we all need to calm down," said Dad as the chair floated by his head and Dyandra jumped onto his shoulders.

It was at that very moment Mr. Bones walked straight into the Dades' kitchen. Everyone screamed.

"Oh! Sorry to startle you," said Mr. Bones. "It's just that

I saw your back door open, and I thought you would want to know. That it was open, I mean." He watched silently as the kitchen chair floated to the ground. A few moments passed as he frowned at it before continuing. "Anyway, er . . . good morning, Dades." His eyes rested on Mom. "Ah, hello there! There's the lady I was talking to you about, Molly! Lovely to meet you properly, and you *must* give me the recipe for your cheese rolls."

"Oh wow," said Timothy. "We are *so* busted."

Grace may have taken the Dades' tale of death and resurrection surprisingly well, but even compared to her, Mr. Bones was miraculously calm. He even chuckled in his strange wheezing way at a few points of their story, his deep-set eyes no longer creepy seeming now that they sparkled with amusement. Molly was beginning to feel increasingly guilty for being so spooked by him.

"Well," he said once they were finished. "I'm very glad you told me. This helps clear up a lot of confusion on my part. And I'll of course not tell another living soul."

"Well, we're all glad you are so understanding about this whole thing," said Mom. "We know it's a *lot*."

"Oh, not at all," said Mr. Bones. "I admit I have a

confession to make, myself." He took a sip of his tea. "You see, I have The Sight."

"Hurgh?" said Dyandra.

"Oh, that just means I see dead people," said Mr. Bones, chucking her under her chin. He narrowly avoided getting bitten. "Just bumbling about, minding their own business normally. My whole family has the gift. We've been haunted by a former matriarch from the eighteenth century as a result."

"Huh, you don't say," said Dad.

"Oh yes," said Mr. Bones. "Old Mother Bones. Had to move to a different continent to get away from her, if I'm being completely honest with you. But yes, dead family members sticking around is something I'm very familiar with. So I know how it goes."

"Wow, Molly and Marty, you owe Mr. Bones an apology," said Dad. "They thought you were up to something."

Mr. Bones wheeze-laughed. "Oh, you did? Whatever for?"

"We, uh, saw you digging that grave with your hands yesterday," said Molly, suddenly very interested in the kitchen floor.

"Ah yes, I can see how that must have looked sinister," said Mr. Bones. "I was just testing a theory of mine."

"A theory?" said Marty.

"Yes. You see that grave . . ." said Mr. Bones, putting down his tea for emphasis, "is an early example of Bartlett Adams!"

"Who?" said everyone except Dad. (Dyandra's sounded more like "Hurgh?")

"He was *only* Maine's first stonemason!" said Dad, now very excited. "There are a few stones in the cemetery I've always suspected are by him."

Mr. Bones nodded. "I quite agree. And not only did I confirm one yesterday, I discovered that it is one of only *four* stones that he signed. He must have made it as a young journeyman when he was still in Boston."

Dad looked utterly thrilled, and everyone else looked utterly confused. "Which grave? Wait, no, don't tell me! Dorcas Larabee. No! Josiah Moffit. Final answer."

Mr. Bones grinned widely. It somehow seemed more dorky than scary now that he was sitting in a sunny kitchen with a cup of tea, which did not ease Molly's guilt. "It was indeed Josiah Moffit! I dug under the burial line on the way home yesterday, and the signature is there, clear as day!"

"Ohhh," said Molly, twisting her hands awkwardly.

"But what about Goody Proxmire's tree?" said Marty. "We uh . . . saw you taking notes by it."

"Oh that!" said Mr. Bones cheerfully. "Well, you see I'm also something of an amateur supernatural historian.

I suppose when you can see ghosts, it makes you curious about the rest. Anyway, I spotted a few more apotropaic marks carved into the tree. You know, like the one we saw in the old crematorium the other night."

"Right . . ." said Molly.

"What's fascinating is whilst most of them look like they've been there a long time, *one* of them looks freshly carved. It's so interesting to see evidence of traditional beliefs carrying over into the present day."

"And these are definitely *anti*-witch marks, right?" said Molly.

"Exactly! Protection against evildoers in general, really," said Mr. Bones.

"Well, I guess that's a relief," said Marty.

"What makes you say that?" said Mr. Bones.

"Molly and Marty think that Goody Proxmire has really cursed them. They also thought that you—" said Timothy before Molly cut him off.

"Finish that sentence and *you will pay,*" Molly hissed quickly. Timothy made a confused face but kept his mouth shut. Fortunately, Mr. Bones hadn't noticed and instead looked as excited as Molly had ever seen him.

"So truly you believe that you have been cursed by a witch?" he said, his pale, thin face now lit up. "That's *wonderful*! I'm so glad to meet someone who can tell me more about current practices in America. Please, tell me, how did you come to this conclusion?'"

"A podcast," said Mom. "Don't worry, we are going to be monitoring them from now on."

"Oh, you must give me the link. I'd love to know more," said Mr. Bones.

"Sure?" said Molly, ignoring her mother's sighs.

"We should probably get to work," said Dad quickly. "It's going to be a busy day. And I *have* to find a way to add that Adams signature to the cemetery tour."

"Oh right," said Mr. Bones, jauntily slapping his thigh before standing up. "Thanks so much for the tea."

"Any time!" said Mom. "It's been so nice having people outside the family to talk to."

As Dad and Mr. Bones headed out of the kitchen, Molly got out her phone and texted Grace.

> It's not Mr. Bones.
> I'll explain later.
> But he's not a vampire . . .
> Just a history nerd.

Chapter
Fourteen

Molly used her sick day listening to *Myth and Westons*, specifically anything they had on witches, with hopes of finding a way to break the curse. Spending hours listening to the graphic descriptions of pustular boils and a victim's nose falling off did little to improve her mood.

Groaning, she rolled over on her bed and tried to focus on what Ethan and Dee were saying.

"In this episode, we are going to be covering Jekylls and Hydes—folks who seem normal, even nice on the outside . . ." said Ethan's mellow voice.

"But are actually harboring dark secrets!" added Dee

gleefully. *"We'll be talking about an IT consultant turned necromancer, a soccer mom who may or may not be a witch, and the twisted tale of a small town teacher's thirst for revenge."*

Molly sighed and paused the podcast. She needed a break.

The late afternoon sun had nearly set and cast long shadows across the cemetery. Molly huddled her jacket closer to her and tried to look for anything out of the ordinary as she walked among the graves. The only thing she could see that fit that description was Dad's headstone Advent calendar.

Molly was starting to feel hopeless. Now that Mr. Bones was ruled out, they didn't have much in the way of clues. Just a whole bunch of freakiness and increasingly severe curse symptoms.

Her arm slamming into someone jolted her out of her thoughts for a moment. "Oh, Mr. Anderson!" she said, flustered. "Sorry, I didn't see you there!"

Mr. Anderson blinked at her, as if he too had been lost in thought. It was always awkward seeing teachers outside of school, mused Molly, but something about this felt extra uncomfortable. As if she wasn't wanted.

"Oh, sorry Molly," he said finally. His voice came out croaky, as if he had been shouting or crying recently. "I was distracted myself."

He nodded to the tomb in front of him. ***ANDERSON*** was written on the side in grand Victorian letters.

"Oh . . . is this your family's?" said Molly. Several families in town had shared tombs like this.

Mr. Anderson nodded. "My parents are buried here. And my brother. And both my sisters."

Molly had a horrible feeling she was giving Mr. Anderson *that look*. She considered smiling politely instead, but it felt inappropriate.

"Oh," she said helplessly. "I . . . uh . . . I'm . . . sorry."

Mr. Anderson didn't seem to notice, as he was back staring at the tomb, shoulders slumped. He nodded, but his mind seemed far away. "You liked my arrangement, didn't you?" he said, so quietly Molly almost didn't hear it.

"I'm sorry?" said Molly again, now confused.

"My arrangement of 'God Rest Ye Merry Gentlemen,'" said Mr. Anderson, his hands now balled into fists. He turned to look at Molly with a strange fire in his eyes. "Because the school board and the superintendent had *things* to say about it. And about the whole music program."

Molly was beginning to realize guiltily that she, or more accurately the curse upon her, was partly responsible for the *things* said. She averted her gaze. Mr. Anderson's knuckles had turned almost white.

"Um, yeah, your arrangement was great!" she said quickly. "I, uh, I'm really sorry I messed it up. At the concert I mean."

Mr. Anderson jolted, and shook his head as if coming

back to reality. "Oh. Oh no, of course not," he said, his eyes returning back to their usual watery expression. "I feel bad, I shouldn't have put pressure on you so close to the first anniversary of . . . *well . . .*"

"Oh, it's okay," said Molly quickly. "It wasn't your fault."

"Still . . ." said Mr. Anderson.

Neither of them seemed to know what to say. An uneasy silence hung in the air for several excruciating moments.

Molly decided this was as good a time as any to back away. "Well, uh . . . bye, Mr. Anderson," she said as she retreated.

"Bye, Molly," said Mr. Anderson, his eyes now fixed back on the tomb. He didn't look up.

Molly was back at school the next day.

Grace had clearly been worried, because she pounced upon Molly the moment Ben left them at the school gates. "How are you feeling? Are you okay?" she gasped, clutching Molly's arms. "Has your hair started falling out yet?"

"I'm okay, I'm fine," said Molly. "Well, not *fine*, but I've been feeling this stuff for a while and no hair loss yet."

When Grace looked skeptical, Molly added to her and Marty, "I promise, if anything happens, I'll let you both know."

"And it will be harder to cover up boils, hallucinations,

body parts falling off, and potential death anyway," added Marty, patting Molly's shoulder. She groaned as Grace's phone beeped.

"This is so unfair. How come Marty gets blown up, I get cursed, Dyandra dies *and* gets turned into a zombie, and Timothy gets *nothing*?" said Molly.

"Maybe whoever's doing this has a crush on him?" said Grace. Molly stared at her. "Um, forget I said anything."

"Do we have any more suspects?" said Marty as Grace's phone beeped again.

"We don't," said Molly. "Grace, did anything out of the ordinary happen at school yesterday?"

"Mr. Anderson got ranting about the school board and superintendent having no respect for the arts," said Grace. "I think they may have sent him another mean email."

"Yeah, he mentioned something about them yesterday," said Molly. "I saw him at the cemetery."

"Wait—he was at the cemetery?" said Marty.

"Yep, at his family tomb," said Molly. "I think all his family might be dead? He seemed pretty upset, but I think that was more to do with the school board not liking his musical arrangements."

"Wait—*all his family are dead?!*" said Marty.

"Yes. Are you repeating me for a reason?" said Molly.

Marty rolled his eyes as Grace's phone beeped. "Okay, so

hear me out, but I think I may have something. I was listening to this *Myth and Westons* episode because it had a soccer mom witch in it—"

"Oh, I listened to that one, too!" said Molly.

"Okay, but did you get to the final story in the podcast? *After* the soccer mom witch?" said Marty.

Molly shook her head.

"So, it was about this theater teacher who had some beef with most of her school. They thought she was this out-of-control mess, she thought they weren't respecting her enough, blah, blah, blah."

"Okay . . ." said Molly. "And did she curse them?"

"No, she tried to set the school on fire in revenge," said Marty. "While everyone was gathered inside watching the school play! Opening night. She made sure that as many people as possible were there. You know, *like Mr. Anderson did for the Christmas concert*!" Molly could feel his eyebrows rising.

"Yes, but, Marty," said Molly. "Why would Mr. Anderson want to set the school on fire? Or, um, do witch stuff to us?"

"Molly's right, Marty," said Grace, looking up from her phone. "What's his motivation? I mean, everything going wrong at the concert has caused a lot of trouble for him. I don't think he's happy about it."

"Well, maybe he was still mad about no one turning up to

last year's concert," said Marty as Grace's phone beeped. "You know, like an 'I'll show you all! You ignore my work, you pull my funding, I'll go out with a bang!' kinda thing. And now he's unhappy because he didn't go far *enough* at the concert. Like he wanted to do worse, but something stopped him!"

"Like an apotropaic mark!" said Molly.

"Ooh, good call," said Marty. Grace's phone beeped again.

"Okay, yes, Marty," said Grace after reading the text. She frowned. "Mr. Anderson *did* freak out in class yesterday. But freaking out doesn't mean he's an evil witch trying to curse us!"

"I dunno, Grace," said Molly. "He did seem pretty . . . intense at the cemetery yesterday. He got a really weird look in his eye when he talked about the school board not liking his work."

"So he felt his art was disrespected? Just like the teacher in the podcast?" said Marty as Grace's phone beeped multiple times. "And you said all his family are dead?"

"Yes, both parents, and all his brothers and sisters."

"Mr. Anderson isn't that old," said Marty to a cacophony of beeps. "Don't you think that's pretty unusual that *all* his siblings are dead? Did he mention *how* they died? And more importantly, *was he there*?"

"No, we didn't get that far. Honestly, it was all really awkward," said Molly.

Grace finished reading Marty's messages and looked up, frowning. "I don't know, Marty. I can't see Mr. Anderson wanting to hurt us. Like, maybe he was at the cemetery because he misses his family, you know? And he'd had a really rough day at work and wanted to be with them."

Her phone beeped again. "I told her it was just a theory," said Marty to Molly. "But one worth looking into."

Molly nodded. "Right. We do need to explore any possible clue or suspect. It's not like we are any closer to finding out who is behind this."

"Fair." Grace sighed. "I guess we could meet up after school at my place? If Ethan and Dee are there, they could give us some more ideas about what to do. It's their last day here, so this is probably our only chance to talk to them."

"We can't," said Molly. "I have a meeting with Ms. Lewis. She wants to meet my dad because she thinks I'm traumatized after the Christmas concert."

"Aww, that's nice. I mean, it's obviously going to be kinda uncomfortable, but—"

"No, it's not that," said Molly. "After our conversation with Mr. Bones went so well, my parents have decided that they will use it to let Ms. Lewis in on the situation."

"So . . . your mom's coming, too?" said Grace.

"Yep," said Molly, grimacing. "I think they're bringing pastries."

Chapter Fifteen

L ater that day, as Molly met her parents in the school hallway, she found out they had brought something far worse than pastries. "Why did you bring Dyandra?" she said weakly.

"We had to, Moll," said Dad as Dyandra chewed his pant leg. Flesh-colored makeup had been poorly applied to her face and part of it had already come off on Dad's leg. "Timothy had a date with Kaitlyn . . ."

"And we don't want you kids to feel you have to put your lives on hold just because some of us are dead," whispered her mom.

"Muuuhhm," said Dyandra.

"Oh sorry, sweetie. Or your *afterlives* on hold either," Mom said a little too loudly. Nearby, several kids looked up, confused. Dyandra snarled at them, and they quickly moved away.

"Okay, let's get this over with," sighed Molly.

The golden late afternoon sun streamed into the classroom as the Dades minus Timothy filed in. Two seats were set before Ms. Lewis's desk, and she greeted them with a smile. "Oh, I see we have one more guest! Let me grab another chair."

"Ah, yes. About that," said Dad. "We actually need *three* more." He strolled over and picked up a couple of stacked chairs.

"Oh! You didn't mention that anyone else was coming," said Ms. Lewis.

"Well, you see, it was kind of hard to explain on the phone," said Mom.

Ms. Lewis dropped the chair she was carrying. Marty caught it just in time to stop it clattering. Spotting the floating chair, Ms. Lewis took a step back. She made a strange squeaking noise and sat on her desk, her hands shaking. "What is *happening*?" she finally spluttered.

"It's kind of a long story," said Mom.

"Right," said Marty, as Ms. Lewis's phone beeped. She checked her phone and made another squeaking noise.

"Are you okay?" said Molly. Ms. Lewis blinked for a few moments, shook herself, and then looked up.

"I think," she said, "you had better start from the beginning."

The Dades did indeed start from the beginning, which meant that the meeting went on long past when everyone else had left the building. After her initial shock, Ms. Lewis seemed, while still startled, at least accepting of the situation. She even agreed to grade Marty's homework, much to Molly's internal dismay.

"Thank you so much for being so understanding," said Mom once they were finished. "I know that our situation is a little . . . unconventional."

"Not at all," said Ms. Lewis. "After teaching at Roehampton for nearly ten years, I've seen families come in all shapes and sizes. And don't worry. I promise to keep this all strictly confidential."

The Dades stood up, put their chairs away if they had corporeal form or poltergeist powers, and finally got ready to leave. Molly rubbed her eyes. It had been a long day.

"Well, if that's everything, I'll see you tomorrow, Molly and Marty," said Ms. Lewis. "Unless there's anything else you want to tell me?" While the Dades looked at one another and shook their heads, they didn't notice Ms. Lewis staring directly at Molly.

On some level, Molly so, *so* wanted to blurt out everything about the curse. About the symptoms she'd been experiencing, the strange things that had been happening, the fears she had for herself and her family.

Instead, she shrugged, and shook her head just like the rest of the Dades. She didn't want Ms. Lewis to dismiss her concerns like her parents had, or seem even weirder to her favorite teacher. And with her parents standing right there, she didn't want to start another argument. Ms. Lewis gave her that almost disappointed look again.

Pins and needles filled Molly's fingertips and toes. They stayed that way the entire ride home.

After dinner, Molly and Marty excused themselves and promised their parents they wouldn't be long. They had agreed to meet Grace at the beach—safely away from any of their families. Grace didn't think it was the right time to fill her dads in on the fact she had been helping her dead friend solve his potential murder, or her living friend's potential cursed status. And since Christmastime was one of the peak seasons at the B&B, there wasn't anywhere they could talk without being disturbed.

Roehampton Beach at night looked like the sort of place that might harbor smugglers or cultists, the lighthouse casting an eerie glare into the mist. Fortunately, the only occupant of the beach that evening was a small gray seal, in that awkward stage between cute cub and fully grown adult. Molly knew exactly how the seal felt.

Grace was already there, shivering against the cold in her puffer jacket. "How did it go?"

"Ms. Lewis took it pretty well . . . eventually," said Molly. "Though now I have to do all my homework, because she's agreed to grade Marty's."

"Wait . . . you've been getting Marty to do your homework?" said Grace as her phone beeped.

"It doesn't matter." Molly sighed. "Did you get to speak to Ethan and Dee?"

"No." Grace shook her head. "I guess 'cause it's their last day, they were out the whole time. But they have their email on their website—we could try messaging them?"

"I already did that. I made it sound like we were talking about the school project, still to be on the safe side," said Molly. "Okay, so our only lead has been ruled out, whoever is doing this might have actually been *in* our house yesterday since the door was open and my lamp exploded, and the only two people we know who could possibly help us might have already left town. Does anyone have any ideas?"

Both Grace and Marty shrugged. Molly sighed, hugging herself. They were doomed.

"Hey, Grace! Hey, Molly!" Molly turned. There, standing like a pair of edgy guardian angels, were Ethan and Dee Weston. They had their bags slung over their shoulders and expensive paranormal investigative equipment in bulky carry cases in each hand.

Stay quiet, texted Molly to Marty as quickly as she could. They have their ghost hunting stuff on them.

Roger that, texted Marty back. He floated several steps back as the girls stepped forward to meet the Westons.

"Hiya! We were just heading out," said Ethan. "Glad we caught you."

"Ethan and I just wanted to say goodbye. We had a blast, and I'm sure our listeners will love our Roehampton episode," said Dee. "And thanks for telling us all about the cemetery and the curse, Molly. Hearing all that lore on the first day was a big help. We'll definitely be using it on our podcast."

"It's been a great trip. The stuff we heard near the graveyard alone ... *man*," said Ethan, grinning as if the restless souls of the dead reaching out to him was a pleasant experience.

Dee nodded. "We definitely caught some unexplained voice phenomena."

"What did it say?" Molly cringed, thinking of Mom.

"Well, it sounded something like 'Helen' or 'Ellen,'" said Ethan. "Or maybe 'melon,' but that would make less sense."

Molly's shoulders sagged with relief. "Oh. Well, that's cool."

"Plus, all this freaky unseasonal weather we've been having. Like that lightning storm the night we arrived," said Dee. "Witches are supposed to cause storms, you know."

Molly's shoulders rose back up. "Oh. Really?"

"Yeah," said Ethan. "We have a theory we'll be going over on *Myth and Westons*—we're wondering if the lightning and the frog shower at the basketball game last year and such are all connected to the upcoming anniversary of the Roehampton witch trials and Goody Proxmire's death."

"You see, everyone here is focusing their collective energy on those two things. We think that it's working kind of like a town-wide séance. And that's causing Goody Proxmire to rise again!" said Dee. "We also believe this may have caused some living witches or acolytes to come out of hiding to enact their revenge. Like perhaps this is all happening because *someone* is casting spells. If you believe in that stuff of course."

"Well, how about that?" said Molly, desperately hoping that the terror she was feeling was not showing on her face. Part of her wanted to tell them the truth about the potential curse—they seemed like they might believe her and could at least give some specific advice.

The problem was, talking openly with Ethan and Dee might land her on their podcast. Even if they didn't use her name, there was only one cursed cemetery in Roehampton, and only one family in town that had lost two members to an explosion in said cursed cemetery. Maintaining a low profile and downplaying any associated weirdness to her classmates would be much harder if they could hear a dramatic account of her cursing online. And if she was perfectly honest with herself, she also liked the Westons' image of her as the sassy skeptic kid.

"Before you guys go, we actually have a few more questions to ask for our . . . school project," said Grace, glancing at Molly and linking arms with her. Molly was once again reminded of why she loved Grace. "So if, hypothetically, someone was cursed by a witch like Goody Proxmire, what could they do to counteract that?"

"Well, first I guess there's always hex apples," said Dee. "Basically, you carve a face on an apple and hang it over a fireplace or a stove to dry out. Or you could keep a clove of garlic or mistletoe in your pocket. Those are some of the more traditional wards at least. The type that the citizens of Roehampton might have used in the time of the witch trials."

"Okay, good to know," said Grace.

"I guess in terms of more general curses, there is the one remedy we featured on *Myth and Westons*," said Ethan. "Episode forty-one: 'Ain't No Grave.'"

"Oh yeah, that's a good one," said Dee. "So we talked to this woman who married the widower of her dead best friend . . . and then freaky stuff started happening. Like *their food rotting overnight in a still-working fridge, blood coming down from the ceiling* freaky."

"They basically had to have a whole apology ceremony at the dead friend's grave, where they promised they had gotten together only *after* she died, and asked for her blessing," said Ethan. "And get this. According to them, as soon as they did that, *everything stopped.*"

"So I guess that means, hypothetically, someone cursed by Goody Proxmire could try apologizing to her grave. Though I don't think you'd be able to reason with her," said Dee, laughing. "I mean, I guess you could *try*. But witches, as far as we can tell, are more like, *Death and destruction to my enemies,* less *Hey let's talk this out.*"

"Right," said Molly as she glanced at Grace. "Well, thanks so much for your help again. But I think we need to get going."

"Yes," said Grace, glancing back. "We need to . . . do a thing."

"Okay, well it was great meeting you both!" said Dee.

"We'll definitely try to return to Roehampton someday," added Ethan. "I actually think we need to take some shots of this beach at night before we go for the Insta feed, Dee. Just *look* at this place."

"Good call," said Dee, taking out her phone. "Bye, Grace and Molly! Good luck with the assignment."

"Thanks!" called out Molly as she and Grace hustled as fast as they could off the beach. "Safe travels!"

Their phones both beeped as they left, but they barely needed to check Marty's message. They all knew where they were going.

Goody Proxmire's hawthorn tree looked even creepier in the dark, which was really quite an achievement. The dark branches twisted and curved almost like they could reach down and snatch any unfortunate soul who happened to pass by. Molly, Marty, and Grace approached slowly. Mr. Bones was right. There were several apotropaic marks on the trunk, and one looked freshly carved.

"Um, what should we say?" said Marty.

Grace's phone beeped. She shrugged as she read the message. "I guess . . . that we're sorry? On behalf of Roehampton?"

"Okay," said Molly, taking a deep breath. "So, uh, Goody Proxmire. Hi."

Suddenly, a group of carolers passed. They quickly quieted down and waited for them to pass. The echoes of *"To save us all from Satan's power, when we had gone astray"* rang through the empty streets until all was still once more.

"As I was saying," Molly started again. "We, uh, wanted to apologize. On behalf of Roehampton."

"We're so sorry that your neighbors turned on you," added Grace. "And that you were executed."

"And that all your friends were put on trial and nearly executed, too," said Molly. "And that they didn't even give you a decent burial, they just put you under this tree."

"And that we now have a tourist industry based around you, and make money off you being this evil witch even though we don't officially believe in witches anymore," said Grace.

"You know," said Marty, "I'm beginning to understand why Goody Proxmire wanted to curse this town."

"Shut up, Marty. This isn't helping," said Molly.

"What did he say?" said Grace.

"Look, all I'm saying is if I were in her position I would be hexing people, too," said Marty as Grace's phone beeped. "Anyway, how do we know if she can even hear me?"

"Uh, she's dead *and* a witch. I think if anyone can hear a poltergeist, she can," said Molly.

"Okay, fair," said Marty. "So . . . yeah. We *are* really sorry, Goody Proxmire."

"*Really* sorry," said Molly. "We wish the people of Roehampton hadn't done that to you. But . . . we're just kids. So, if you could maybe lift the curse, I don't know, that would be awesome."

"We are genuinely really sorry this happened to you," added Marty. "That was really messed up, but cursing us won't change that."

"I'm so sorry for everything, Goody Proxmire," said Molly. "Please don't let me get boils, or have my hair fall out, or my nose fall off, or any of that stuff. And call off anyone who is maybe trying to curse me in your name."

"Like Mr. Anderson," said Marty.

"We promise to make you sound really nice in our school project," said Grace. "And let everyone know how wrong what Roehampton did to you was."

"Yeah, definitely," said Molly.

Silence hung in the air. No one seemed to know what else to say.

"Do we think that did anything?" said Grace hopefully.

Molly looked around. She didn't know what she was expecting. Maybe some change in the atmosphere, or a comforting rustling of the branches to let them know that they were forgiven. Instead, there was no indication that anyone had even been listening.

"I'm not sure," said Molly. "And I guess we all need to get back soon or our parents will freak out."

"Yeah," said Grace. "Let's sleep on it. Maybe some rest will help us work out what to do next."

Chapter
Sixteen

But that night, Molly could barely sleep again. Her dreams were haunted by witches and great hawthorn trees trapping her in their roots. She tried to scream for help, but no sound came out. Then every time Molly awoke, she tossed and turned fretfully and rearranged herself on her bed.

Her alarm woke her with a start, merely moments after she finally managed to peacefully drift off. The bulb in her bedside table light had been replaced, but Molly didn't dare turn it on. Instead, she used the light in her phone to guide herself, half awake at best, out of bed, into her clothes, and through her bedroom door. Marty was cautiously entering the hallway, too, even more sullen than he was most mornings.

They headed silently into the kitchen together, past the hex apples laid out on the stove that they had carved the night before. Molly had tried to make the face she carved on her apple as cute and friendly as possible. It hadn't worked, and it squint-grimaced at her menacingly. Marty's apple meanwhile was charming—he had always been good with his hands, and no longer having them had somehow not stopped him.

All around them, the rest of the Dades bustled about. It was Timothy's turn to put in Dyandra's mouth guard this morning, and she was behaving beautifully, as she always did with him. She gave him a winning neon-pink smile as he high-fived her.

Having confirmed that her family was not paying attention, Molly sneaked into the pantry. She grabbed a clove of garlic and shoved it in her pocket. "Something else Ethan and Dee suggested," she whispered to Marty who had followed her. He nodded.

The doorbell tolled, and for a change Molly didn't wince. It meant that Grace and one of her dads would be here to take her to school. Away, at least for a little while, from her cursed house.

The pins and needles returned to her hands. She rubbed one on the garlic for good luck.

It was the last day before winter break, one of those sleepy ones filled with goofy half-lessons that no one is graded on. Molly glided through it all in a daze. On the one hand, with everyone still whispering about the Christmas concert she had never been gladder for a semester to end. On the other hand, school seemed like it could be safer, or at least not as officially cursed as her own home right now.

Making things weirder, Cara had been staring at her all day. Molly was used to Cara's glares, but normally Cara stuck her nose in the air and looked away right afterward, or whispered something mean to a friend. This was different. Cara was looking at Molly like she was considering something, and she wasn't looking away. Even Cara's friends noticed and nudged Cara occasionally in an attempt to get her to snap out of it.

Molly tried to shrug it off. She needed to focus on breaking the curse, not dumb Cara. "I was looking online," she said to Grace and Marty at lunch. "And apparently people used to bury shoes under doors and chimneys to keep out witches and evil spirits. Basically entranceways."

"Okay, I've got a couple of pairs I've grown out of," said Grace. Her phone beeped.

"I told Grace she should bury those outside the doors to her place, just in case," said Marty to Molly. "We can use my shoes for ours. It's not like I can wear them anymore."

The rest of the school day passed mostly uneventfully, apart from Cara's stares and Mr. Anderson nearly crying when describing the newest strongly worded email sent to him by the school superintendent about cutting the music program's event funding completely. Even though he was still a suspect, this made Molly feel extremely guilty about the Christmas concert debacle all the same. Marty elbowing her and giving her knowing, if invisible, looks in Mr. Anderson's direction did not help either.

Thankfully, lessons ended early due to Mr. Anderson fleeing class. Molly was just about to head out with Grace, when Cara grabbed her arm.

"Can we talk privately?" said Cara, her large brown eyes strange and intense. "There's something I need to tell you."

"What?" said Molly as she pulled her arm back.

Cara looked around. "I can't tell you here. Just trust me."

It was Molly's turn to stare. She *didn't* just trust Cara. Besides, she had things to do and curses to break. Then she heard Marty whisper in her ear.

"Just go with her, Moll. I'm curious. And I'll stay with

you so there's backup if she tries anything. But not in an obvious poltergeist way," he added quickly.

"Okay, fine," said Molly.

"I'll wait for you," said Grace.

Cara nodded and turned. Molly followed as Cara led the way down several deserted corridors to a secluded and empty classroom. She opened the door and gestured to Molly to enter.

Molly looked at her for a moment. Something about this didn't feel right. Not only was Cara definitely acting suspicious, she had been the first person Molly had thought of as someone who would want to curse her. Back when she and Marty still thought it was probably Mr. Bones.

And she'd let Marty talk her out of her suspicions so quickly. Molly hoped that wasn't a mistake, but she stepped into the room anyway. She couldn't think what else to do.

Once Molly was in, Cara leaned out of the door frame and looked left and right as if to make sure no one had followed. Which was both weirdly dramatic, and since Marty had already sneaked in behind her, too late. More strangeness.

"So, what do you have to tell me?" Molly said as Cara shut the door firmly. She turned to Molly and took a deep breath.

"Okay, so I was—" Cara stopped and sniffed the air, frowning. "Is that . . . is that *garlic*?"

Molly felt the clove in her pocket. It had gotten a little battered throughout the school day, and pungent fumes had followed her around since third period. "What? No!" said Molly, the pins and needles returning to her hands. "Anyway, you were saying?"

Cara sniffed the air again and shrugged. "Well. All right, so . . ."

The pins and needles had spread to Molly's feet now and were traveling down her limbs and up her spine. She felt the familiar lurch of her stomach just as her ears started ringing.

"Are you okay?" said Cara suspiciously. Just like that day at the library before the first violin chair audition. When Molly had also felt the pins and needles . . . right after sitting next to Cara.

Molly gasped. She had felt that same dizziness and ringing in her ears at the audition for the Christmas concert . . . when Cara was watching from the front row.

And then at the Christmas concert itself, where she felt *all* the symptoms and then *everything* happened . . . when Cara was sitting right next to her in the violin section.

In fact, her symptoms had always been particularly bad around Cara. And now, just as Cara had gotten her all alone—or at least alone as far as Cara knew—suddenly all of Molly's curse symptoms were coming on at once. She leaned against a desk to counteract the dizziness. Then the lights started flickering.

Molly looked back at Cara, who was gazing up at the lights, which started crackling and spitting violently. Then, slowly, like some mechanical doll, Cara lowered her head and stared at Molly with a cold, unreadable look in her eyes. She seemed almost angry.

The silence was broken by a strange metallic *screeeeeeeech* to Molly's left. Then another screech, this time to her right, and then more screeches behind her.

Molly felt the desk she was leaning on punt her forward. She stumbled and spun around to see all the chairs and desks in the classroom suddenly arranged in a half circle, pointing toward her and Cara. They seemed almost like a pack . . . waiting to pounce. Molly backed away toward the door.

"Ahhh!" she yelped as she was propelled forward by the door suddenly swinging open. Regaining her balance, Molly heard the sickening metallic screech again. The chairs and desks moved again, sliding toward her and gaining speed. Like they were charging. Behind her, the door slammed shut and swung wildly open, over and over, so fast that Molly couldn't escape. Cara started opening her mouth.

Just then, two ghostly hands grabbed Molly from under her armpits and lugged her out of the room before she could hear what Cara was going to say . . . or what spell she was going to deliver. Molly could feel Marty bracing the door open as he pulled her through. It slammed firmly shut behind them.

"Molly! Moll!" said Marty, setting her on the floor once they were safely out of the room. "Can you run? I can carry you, but it'll slow us down." She nodded shakily.

The two sprinted and floated through the halls, then out of the school building as fast as they could. Grace was waiting for them by the entrance. Molly shot a quick look over her shoulder before bending over, wheezing to catch her breath. They hadn't been followed. Yet.

"Are you okay?" said Grace. "What did Cara want to tell you?"

Molly shook her head and gasped.

"It's her!" she said between gulping breaths. "Cara's the witch! And she's *after me*!"

Chapter Seventeen

Molly, Grace, and Marty caught the last school bus just in time. They watched Roehampton Middle School retreat far into the distance, with no sign of Cara, before anyone dared to speak. Grace's phone started beeping furiously with Marty's explanation of what happened.

"We should head to the beach," said Molly. "We need to make sure no one can hear us."

Roehampton Beach had a few dog walkers strolling up and down the sand, so they held back and sat on a nearby bench.

"I realized it while I was in the room with Cara," said Molly, once they were sure no one was listening but a couple of predatory seagulls. "Every single time I've been near her since my symptoms started, they've gotten worse."

"Why didn't you say anything?" said Grace.

"Well, before a few days ago I thought it was just stress, and well, Cara stresses me out!" said Molly. "But now I realize it's because of a curse. . . . I dunno, doesn't it make sense that if Cara was trying to cast a spell on someone, she'd pick me? I mean, even *without* the fact I live in a cursed house."

"But isn't Cara a descendant of a witch *hunter*, not a witch?" said Marty as Grace's phone beeped. "It's kind of weird she's turned out to be a witch herself."

"Not really," said Molly. "Ms. Lewis is a descendant of a witch hunter *and* Goody Proxmire, right? So who's to say that Cara hasn't got some spookiness in her family alongside Reverend Hartman? Maybe she didn't mention her witch ancestor to throw us off the scent? You know, because she's trying to curse us!"

"I guess that makes sense," said Grace. "But still, that means that Cara killed Marty *and* your mom. She's a terrible person, don't get me wrong, but I never thought she was *murder* bad."

"Isn't that what they say any time they catch a murderer?" said Molly. "The neighbors are always like, 'Oh, they were so nice and normal seeming, I can't believe they're a serial killer.' And Cara isn't even *nice*!"

"I guess . . ." said Grace, still looking unsure. "But what can we do to prove it? Or even better, stop her before she does anything else?"

Molly shrugged and shook her head. "I guess we look for something. . . ." She and Grace pulled out their phones and opened their web browsers.

Finding search terms that returned decent results about how to protect yourself from a classmate who is a witch and may want to kill you was difficult enough. It was made even harder in Molly's case by Marty.

"Try 'what to do if witch with real magic is trying to curse me'?" he suggested. "No! 'Killer curse witch classmate protection.'"

"Stop directly typing at the same time as me!" said Molly. "You're confusing my phone."

Marty shrugged. "I'm quicker than you."

"And now you're scrolling down too fast for me to read! Just let me do it!" said Molly.

"Well, you're taking forever!"

"Well, I don't trust your suggestions!" snapped Molly. "You thought Mr. Anderson was the witch, when he really was just upset about work and his dead family. *And* you talked me out of suspecting Cara, when she was the actual witch!"

"Okay, and I feel really bad about that," said Marty.

"But I'm still *definitely* better than you at typing and search terms."

"You are *not*!" said Molly.

"Um . . . are you guys okay?" said Grace.

"We're fine!" said Molly as Grace's phone beeped several times. Grace took a quick glance at it, held up her hands, and looked away.

After scouring the internet like this for over an hour, the kids found nothing. Or at least nothing practical from any source that looked trustworthy. (They did, however, find several sites selling crystals for extortionate prices they could not afford.) It was also getting increasingly cold and dark. Dejected, Molly, Marty, and Grace decided to head home and try again tomorrow.

"We'll think of something, Molly, don't worry," said Grace.

"She's right," said Marty "I'm not sure *what* yet, but there's got to be *something*."

Molly wished she could believe them.

Still, another night passed, and nothing exploded in Molly's room. Molly's dreams, however, remained terrifying. This time they featured desks swarming and crushing her, chairs aiming their legs at her face like blunt metal pincers. She staggered out of her room the next morning, exhausted, spaced out, and not in the mood to do anything.

"Has anyone seen my keys to the crematorium?" said Dad as she lurched into the kitchen. "The Sullivans are here, and they need me to show them how to work the Kremragende again."

Molly rubbed her eyes and yawned. Sullivan & Son & Grandson were Roehampton's premier, and also only, morticians. As Mike Sullivan was 58, Jim Sullivan was 79, and Pat Sullivan a spritely 101, the workings of Dad's fancy new Danish cremation furnace was beyond them. This was the fifth time they had requested a tutorial, which Dad didn't mind at all since the Kremragende Eco Furnace was his current favorite topic of conversation.

"When did you last see the keys?" asked Mom. Behind her, Marty slumped into the kitchen, acting as listless as Molly felt.

"A few days ago," said Dad as he scratched his head. "They should be on the hook by the kitchen door like the rest of them."

Molly looked up, suddenly fully awake. That door had been left open the morning her bedside lamp exploded, when Mr. Bones walked in on them. This was more evidence someone else really had been in the house that night. What other things could Cara have done while they slept?

"I guess I can get a new set cut from Mr. Bones's copy,

and he can let the Sullivans in now," said Dad. "I won't get another chance to show them before the next funeral with Christmas coming up."

"Dad, can we listen in on your tutorial?" said Molly. "I know I would like to know more about the Kremen-regard thingy."

"Kremragende," said Dad, beaming. "Of course you can! I'd *love* to show you more about it any time! You should have said so earlier!"

"Well, you know . . ." said Molly, shrugging.

"You always seemed so bored when we talked about it before, I thought you weren't interested!" continued Dad. "Like when you called it the Swedish furnace, and I told you it was actually a *Danish* furnace, using the latest energy-saving technology while not sacrificing efficiency, and you said 'Whatever.'"

"Oh, noooo, I would definitely like to take a look at it," said Molly. "Marty, too, *right*?" she said, turning and raising her eyebrows at her twin.

"Yeah . . . sure?" said Marty to his dad. He turned to Molly. *"Why?"* he hissed in her ear. *"Last time we got near that thing, Dad spent thirty minutes going over the different temperature settings."*

Molly got out her phone and texted him so Dad wouldn't hear.

I think the keys to the crematorium went missing the
night the back door was left open and my lamp exploded.
Which means Cara could have taken them. What if she is
trying to blow the rest of us up using the new furnace?

Marty's invisible eyes widened as he read the message
over Molly's shoulder. "I mean, yeah definitely, Dad!" he
said, his voice suddenly bright and enthusiastic. "I'd really
like you to tell us *all* about the Kremagrendel."

"Kremragende," said Dad.

"Right, yes, that," said Marty. "Specifically, if you could
tell us all about how it *works*."

"Ah, good to see we have a younger Dade," said Mr. Bones
when they reached the crematorium.

"Mart—uh, just Molly wanted to know more about the
Kremragende," said Dad. "Watch out, Sullivans, it looks like
there might be another family in the burial business in town!"

The Sullivans were already there, arranged in age order,
which also happened to be reverse height order. Tiny, old
Pat Sullivan stood closest to the crematorium door, like the
first step on a human staircase. "Ayuh," he said, looking not
at all worried at the prospect of the Dades as competition.

Meanwhile, Mr. Bones unlocked the doors to the new crematorium, built from layers of cinder block and brick. It was built to withstand a hurricane, after the previous crematorium's roof had been torn off by one. He turned on the light, the cheap fluorescent tubes taking a while to fully send the room out of darkness. "I'll be listening in, too, if you don't mind. I could do with a refresher on the Kremi . . . Krema . . . er, on the furnace," he said.

Molly got a text from Marty.

I'm going inside the kremawhatever.

I want to check everything is looking like it should.

Like it hasn't got any obvious cursed parts or something.

Molly nodded and watched as her brother slid into the machinery. Mr. Bones saw her looking and elbowed her. "I take it there's a *ghost in the machine*?" he whispered in a way that implied that this was a joke.

"Yes?" said Molly, confused. "Marty just wants to see how it works from the inside." She turned back to Dad, who was just starting up his lecture.

It was somehow even *more* boring than she was expecting. Molly felt her cheeks burning from smiling in an attempt to look interested. She dug her fingernails into her palms, hoping the pain would keep her awake. Dad went into *great* detail about how the system worked. The Sullivans seemed to understand everything, and even asked questions that made sense to Dad, but it might as well have been in ancient Sumerian to Molly.

Then Dad went into even worse detail about the "intuitive touch screen." Molly didn't need a tutorial to understand that, but evidently the Sullivans did. At one point, Pat asked Dad what a space bar was.

After Dad explained to the Sullivans for the sixth time how to go back a page, Marty slipped out of the furnace. "It all looks good," he said in a low enough voice that Dad would not hear. "No sign of any normal tampering, let alone any witch-based tampering."

"Do you know what witch-based tampering looks like?" said Molly in an equally low voice, glancing quickly at Dad. He was busy trying to show Jim Sullivan how to tap the touch screen to life.

"Well . . . no," admitted Marty. "I'm just saying— *What is that*?"

Molly looked to where Marty's invisible hand was pointing. There, scratched roughly into the side of the furnace, was another apotropaic mark.

"But these are for protection *against* witches! This doesn't make any sense," said Molly, running her fingers across the surface, her mind racing. "Why would Cara want to protect us from *herself*?"

"Unless it wasn't Cara who took the keys," said Marty. "What if it was someone else trying to protect us from *her*? Or—"

"Oh, have you found another apotropaic mark?" said Mr. Bones, from behind them. Molly and Marty yelped. "Oh dear, sorry to startle you, but this is *fascinating*."

Molly suddenly remembered that Mr. Bones had described himself as an "amateur supernatural historian." Which sounded exactly like the sort of person that could help them defeat Cara. Why hadn't she thought of it before? Molly was about to ask him to tell her more, when she realized that Dad had finally noticed them gathering around the mark.

"What's fascinating, Bones?" he said as he walked over to them and the eerie carving. "And— WHAT HAPPENED TO THE NICE SCANDINAVIAN ENAMEL?!"

"We just found it, Dad," said Molly. "Maybe it was done by the person that took your keys?"

"Oh, you'll be able to fix that up, no problem," said Pat. "You'll just want to clean it, take off the rough edges with some fine-grit sandpaper, and then fill it in with epoxy. . . ."

Dad looked at him with a mixture of relief and gratitude, like Pat was a doctor telling him that his disease was treatable.

With Dad distracted, Molly turned to Mr. Bones. He was still looking at the mark, shaking his head.

"Someone went to a lot of trouble to put that here—especially in a room that's normally locked," he said. "This is the best example of classic superstitions carried into the modern world that I've found! Aside from you two and your curse preventions of course."

"Actually, Mr. Bones," said Molly, checking Dad wasn't listening. "Marty and I wanted to talk to you about that."

Chapter
Eighteen

Mr. Bones agreed to go with them immediately, eager to talk some more about witchcraft and lore. "And to be perfectly honest with you, I don't think I need the touch screen explained in *that* much detail."

Molly had thought they could find a quiet corner of the graveyard to talk, but they were waylaid almost immediately by Mom. She was smiling dreamily into the gray December skies, looking frail and vulnerable against the Maine winter cold, still dressed in only her kaftan.

"The sky merging into the horizon through that mist is just *so* inspiring," she exclaimed. "And the way it's framed by the trees . . . Marty, could you help me make a canvas later?"

"Sure, Mom," said Marty. "But we're helping Mr. Bones . . . uh . . . make some tea?"

"Oh, that's sweet of you!" said Mom. "Nice to see you, Mr. Bones!"

"Lovely seeing you, too, Julia!" called Mr. Bones. "Glad that you're not letting a lack of corporeal form hold you back!"

As they crossed the cemetery to the Dades' house, Molly brooded on her parents. Dad seemed more concerned about his dumb furnace than Cara potentially breaking in to kill them all, or at least give them boils. And Mom was just as spacey as ever, even in the face of impending further doom. Why did they have to be so goofy and so in denial that they were in serious danger? What was *wrong* with her family?

Once they reached the house, Molly stopped. She could see shadows through the back door that led into the kitchen. Her heart started racing, and the dizziness and pins and needles returned. Was Cara here now?

She held her breath and opened the back door. There, sitting on the counter, was Timothy with Marty's hex apple in his hand and Dyandra with Molly's hex apple in hers. Both their mouths were full, and both of the hex apples were half eaten.

"What are you *doing*?" spluttered Molly in outrage.

Dyandra held up her half-eaten apple triumphantly, the awkward face Molly carved into it now missing an eye.

"Braaaaaaaiiiiins!" she said.

"I'm *so* sorry, guys, I didn't realize they were that important to you," said Timothy after Molly had stopped yelling. "I just thought they were some weirdly creepy Christmas decorations! Then Dyandra ate one, and I figured they were going to expire if they were left out like that anyway, so we should just eat them now. . . ."

Molly sighed. Sometimes Timothy could be impossible to stay mad at. "It's okay. We can make some more."

"You sure? I can help!" said Timothy.

"That . . . will be okay," said Molly. Timothy had a tendency to get distracted by anything that wasn't basketball, and she didn't trust him around sharp knives. A few Halloweens ago he'd landed in the ER after pumpkin carving with a tiny dollar-store tool. "But thank you."

Mr. Bones had somehow already made a cup of tea and was settled down at the kitchen table with it. "So, you wanted to ask me something about apotropaic practices?"

"If that is anti-witch stuff, then yes, we do," said Molly.

"Some weird stuff happened at school yesterday. We're now pretty sure the witch trying to fulfill Goody Proxmire's curse is a classmate of ours. And we wanted to know what we could do to stop her, or at least protect ourselves."

"Which classmate?" said Timothy.

"Cara Hartman," said Molly. "Anyway, we—"

"Wait, now you think *Cara Hartman* is in league with Goody Proxmire? Last week it was Mr.—"

"Shut UP!" said Molly. She glanced over at Mr. Bones, who sipped his tea quietly in the corner, politely avoiding their gazes.

"I'm just saying, when is this going to stop, Moll?" said Timothy. "Scary apples, okay, fine, sure. But going around accusing people, saying they are trying to curse us is weird *and* mean! Who are you going to accuse next? Kaitlyn?" Timothy stopped suddenly. "That's a joke, Moll. Please don't accuse my girlfriend of being a witch."

"Oh, she's your *girlfriend* now?" said Marty.

Timothy grinned and looked down, suddenly shy, which was not like him at all. "Yeah, we became official last night." He was actually blushing.

"Oh, that's lovely," said Mr. Bones.

"Yes, very lovely, but I'm *serious* about Cara, Tim," said Molly. "I know I don't have proof right now, but I didn't think to get my phone out in that particular moment seeing as she *was literally making desks and chairs charge at me.*"

"Well, maybe she's got a poltergeist relative, too?" said Timothy, taking another bite of apple.

"Ooh, I didn't think of that one," said Marty.

"Because that doesn't explain *everything*," said Molly. "Like, what about my curse symptoms or the apotropaic marks? This all points to a witch!"

Timothy sighed. "Okay, whatever, I know I can't convince you. Just . . . don't do anything *weird* to Cara." He picked up Dyandra. "Come on, Dy-Dy, let's go chase some squirrels."

"Squuirrrrl braaaaains!" said Dyandra.

After watching her living and mostly living siblings leave the kitchen, Molly turned back to Mr. Bones. "So, what would you do if you seriously thought a witch had cursed you? As an amateur lore expert, I mean."

Mr. Bones took a sip of his tea. "Hmm, well, hex apples are new to me. I'm more familiar with burying old shoes by the doors to your house where I'm from. Or hiding them in chimneys. Basically, any possible entryway."

"Okay, we've already done that," said Molly.

"Oh wonderful!" said Mr. Bones. "You could always take it a step further then and try a dead, dried-out cat buried in the same place." He took another sip of tea. "The nice thing about dead cats is you can also leave them under your bed in a pinch, and they should do the same job as the shoes. But more specific to the cursed person."

"Good to know," said Marty.

Molly shuddered.

"And I suppose this is a bit more complicated," said Mr. Bones, "but you could also try a witch bottle."

"Great," said Molly, happy to hear a solution they hadn't tried and also didn't sound horrifically creepy. "What are those?"

"Oh, they are these small filled and sealed bottles that you bury by an entrance to a house, or in the roof, foundation, or walls to protect the inhabitants," said Mr. Bones. "We had one hidden in the thatching in the house I grew up in."

"So when you say 'filled and sealed,'" said Marty, "filled with what exactly?"

Mr. Bones took another thoughtful sip of tea. "The ingredients vary, but typically they would have included things like rosemary and other herbs, sand, maybe some seawater, knotted thread, some silver charms perhaps." As he spoke, Molly scrawled it all down on a spare pad of paper. "Oh, and a piece of the victim of the curse."

"A . . . piece of the victim?" said Molly, not liking where this was going.

"Oh yes. Anything will do—hair, fingernails, saliva. Or, erm, *excretions*," said Mr. Bones. "The piece of the victim is the most important part; it's essential for an antidote against a witch's curse."

"Good to know," said Molly. "Anything else?"

"Well, if we're being very strict about this, a witch bottle should be prepared by a good witch, or perhaps a local wise woman. If you want them to be fully effective, that is. It's a bit of a 'takes a thief to catch a thief' sort of job."

"Okay, but we don't know any good witches or local wise women," said Molly. "Or at least, I don't think we do. The only witch we know is *definitely* evil."

"Yes, I can see how that is a problem," said Mr. Bones. "Quite frankly, people back in those days might not have had access to anyone like that either. I suggest you do what they would have done and just prepare one yourself. Just seal all the ingredients in a small bottle, conceal it in an appropriate place in your house, and voilà! There's your witch bottle!"

"Okay. That doesn't seem too bad. I guess we can try that," said Molly. "Thanks, Mr. Bones, you were a big help!"

"Oh, no problem at all," said Mr. Bones as he finished his tea and stood up. "I should get back to work myself. Best of luck with everything!"

As Molly and Marty left the kitchen, she sent Grace a text:

> Are you free tomorrow morning? Mr. Bones gave us a recipe for an anti-witch bottle we can try.

> We'll need to get some ingredients together. I warn you, they're weird.

Chapter
Nineteen

After remaking the hex apples, sourcing the ingredients for the witch bottles, and helping Mom with dinner and Christmas wrapping, the rest of the day had gotten away from Marty and Molly. It was time to turn in for the night.

Remembering Mr. Bones's advice, Molly also grabbed the Dades' late pet cat that Mom had taxidermied years ago from the foyer. He was one of Mom's first attempts and not her best. Molly tried not to look at his face, now frozen in an eternal grimace of rage, as she moved him into her room.

After pulling out an impressive amount of junk from

under her bed, Molly placed the stuffed cat there. He just about fit if she laid him sideways. "Sorry, Greebo," she whispered as she got into bed, doubtful that this would do anything.

However, to her surprise, Molly awoke the next day to sunlight streaming in through the windows. She blinked, barely able to believe it. The pins and needles were gone, as was the dizziness. And because she'd actually slept through the night, she felt rested for the first time in a long while.

Molly bounded out of bed, just in time to see Marty leave his room. "I can't believe this," she said, "but I actually think the dead cat worked. Mr. Bones was right!"

Marty gave her an invisible high five. "That's awesome. Maybe once we make the witch bottles, we'll be all set. And then no one will get blown up this Christmas!"

They met Grace at the beach not long after. She waved to Molly and held up her bag of small bottles and jars. "One for every exit at the B-and-B. Thanks to the fire code, that's a lot."

"Okay, great," said Molly, holding up her own bottles. "And you have something from every family member in each of them?"

"Yep, I pulled hair from my dads' hairbrushes, and it's got my hair in there, too," said Grace.

"Perfect," said Molly. "We couldn't find any silver charms at such short notice, but we have everything else apart from the sand and seawater in ours."

"Same," said Grace as they walked toward the shore. "And you said Mr. Bones said that witch bottle ingredients vary, right?"

"Exactly," said Molly. "So I don't think that matters. Let's get that sand and seawater and then bury these bottles!"

"I packed a measuring jug," said Marty. "So you don't have to dunk the bottles and lose any ingredients."

"Aw, nice!" said Molly as she pulled the jug out of the bag. "Thanks, Marty, good idea." She bent down into waves lapping the shore with the jug. The water frothed and bubbled around her boots before receding.

"Molly . . ." said Grace.

"One moment, Grace, I'm just getting the seawater," said Molly as she filled her jug. "Oooh, it's wicked cold!"

"No, seriously, Molly," said Marty, "you need to look up. Like *right now*!"

Molly did, and saw what her friend and her brother were staring at. There, standing halfway down the beach, dressed all in black, was Cara Hartman. Watching them.

The pins and needles returned to Molly's hands, her ears

started ringing, and her stomach started doing loops. She grabbed Grace's arm to steady herself, the seawater sloshing out of the jug she held in her other hand. Cara slowly tilted her head to one side, not breaking eye contact.

"Oh! Hi, Cara! Didn't see you there!" said Molly, forcing a smile while she tried to think of an appropriate thing to say to a witch who has recently thrown furniture at you and probably wants to curse you to death. "Uh . . . how's it going?"

Cara just stood there, her mouth a thin, tight line, and her large dark eyes strangely fierce. They remained fixed on Molly.

"Good," she said after an ominous pause.

"Okay, great!" said Molly. "Us too!" Cara still hadn't moved, and was still staring. Molly suddenly felt very aware of the witch bottles she was holding suspiciously in her hands. She shifted from foot to foot and looked at Grace.

"Uh, we actually need to get back to doing this um . . . thing with these . . . uh . . . bottles," said Grace. "But it was nice seeing you, Cara! Merry Christmas!"

There was another ominous pause. "Merry Christmas," said Cara finally, but with enough venom to make it sound like a swear word.

The wind picked up again, making Molly's eyes water. Cara's long black coat whipped around, looking like strange dark wings. Remembering what the Westons had told her about witches and storms, Molly shuddered. She was glad for the new clove of garlic currently stinking up her much shabbier, but less spooky-looking jacket.

Then, just as suddenly as she'd appeared, Cara turned and walked in the opposite direction across the beach. Molly's pins and needles receded, and the wind died down. Molly, Marty, and Grace looked at one another silently as Cara retreated into the distance, and they didn't start working on their witch bottles again until she was safely out of sight.

"Let's finish up," said Molly, her hands trembling as she poured the seawater from the jug into the bottles that Grace held.

"She turned up just as we were making something to protect ourselves from her," said Marty. "I don't like it. Like, did she know what we were going to do? Is that why she seemed so mad?"

"I'm too freaked out to talk about that right now, Marty," said Molly. Grace looked up but for once didn't ask what Marty said.

Once Molly and Grace had added water and sand to every single one of their bottles and jars, they sealed them as quickly as they could and threw them back into their bags. Meanwhile, Marty kept lookout.

"We should go," he said as Grace's phone beeped. "I don't want to stick around in case Cara decides to come back."

"He's right," said Grace, shifting her now much heavier bag on her shoulder. "And we've got a *lot* of bottles to bury."

They got to work, and sure enough, burying all of Grace's bottles took much longer than they expected, especially with the added challenge of dodging B-and-B guests. By the time Molly and Marty had finished burying their own at every entrance point to the Dades' house, their time had run out for any further research.

Because on top of everything, 'twas the night before Christmas now. Molly had hoped, with two family members not eating, there would be less to do this year. However, with a new zombie sibling and a guest to impress in the form of Mr. Bones, this was not the case. Molly spent the rest of the evening peeling several pounds of potatoes and helping to brine the turkey under the watchful ghostly eyes of her mother.

Still, as she went to bed that night, Molly felt a little better. She even rubbed the dead cat's head for good luck. Sure, Cara had been creepy today . . . but their precautions had worked the night before. Maybe she just looked mad because she saw they had found a way to break her curse? Which meant that their hex apples, witch bottles, and dead cat just might do the trick. Molly felt herself begin to drift off to sleep. Maybe it was all going to be okay.

Chapter
Twenty

Molly awoke on Christmas morning with the sun shining on her face again. She stretched and smiled, happy to have another full night's sleep.

After dressing in the least terrible of several Christmas sweaters that circulated among the Dades, Molly headed downstairs to the kitchen. On her way there she bumped into Marty.

"Hey, Moll!" he said brightly. "Merry Christmaaaa—AAARGH, MOLLY, WHAT IS ON YOUR FACE?!"

Molly gasped and ran to the bathroom, with Marty close behind her. She peered into the old distressed mirror that hung over the vanity. There, red, angry, and taking up increasing amounts of her chin, was a real-life pustular boil just like Ethan and Dee described. The next stage of being cursed by a witch.

"I don't understand it," she gasped, staring at her reflection in horror. "All our precautions worked the night before last. And now we have witch bottles buried outside, so shouldn't that be *more* protection? What happened? Have Cara's powers *grown* or something?" Molly's mouth filled with saliva as if she was about to puke as her stomach lurched and flipped. The lights flickered above them and in the hallway.

"Maybe that's why Cara was down at the beach yesterday," said Marty as they fled the bathroom. "Like she *knew* somehow what we were doing and then followed us to jinx our witch bottles while we were making them."

"Do you think we should, I dunno, unbury them?" said Molly. She didn't continue, because at that moment their mom floated out to greet them.

"Merry Christmas!" she said, enfolding them in a cold, spectral almost embrace. She startled when she saw Molly's face. "Oh, sweetie, that's a big pimple. Do you want to pop it?"

"It's not a pimple and *no*!" said Molly desperately.

"Okay, well, Dad's already got the turkey in," continued Mom, "so I thought we could open our presents before Mr. Bones arrives."

"Uh, we actually need to do something first, Mom," said Molly, looking at Marty.

"Can it wait? We won't have much time later," said Mom. "Not with everything we need to do to get food on the table."

"The jinxed bottles were just a theory," said Marty into Molly's ear. "I don't think we need to do anything to them right now."

"What's this about bottles?" said Mom.

"Oh, nothing important," said Molly quickly. "Uh . . . let's open the presents!" Marty shrugged at her. It looked like the witch bottles, and any possible antidotes to Cara's curse, would have to wait.

A few hours later, the witch bottles were still waiting. The Dades' kitchen at Christmastime was as chaotic as it had been when everyone was still alive. There was something strangely comforting in that, and Molly needed all the comfort she could get when a witch's curse was currently throbbing on her lower face. (Timothy had offered one of his Korean zit stickers for it, which did not help her mood.)

The doorbell tolled as mournfully as ever. Dad ran to answer and returned to the kitchen with Mr. Bones, who today wore a green sweater with an elf on it. He was carrying a box under one arm and a tray covered with foil in his hands. "Merry Christmas, everyone!" he said as he put down his gifts on the kitchen table. "I brought Christmas crackers, and mince pies for pudding. I mean, *dessert*."

"Braaaaains!" said Dyandra as she lifted the foil off the tray.

"Well, not quite." Mr. Bones chuckled. "Though they aren't vegetarian." Molly and Marty looked at each other.

"I'm so glad you could make it," said their mom.

"Oh, thank you so much for having me, Julia," said Mr. Bones. "I don't have any family in this country after the divorce, and I didn't really fancy going back home to answer questions about my failed marriage from Old Mother Bones." He wheeze-laughed.

Seeing that her parents were distracted, Molly used the opportunity to text Grace a photo of her boil. She'd just managed to hit send on a follow-up message of !!!!!! when Dad noticed what she was doing.

"Hey, Moll, it's Christmas and we have a guest. Time to put your phone away."

"But, Dad—" protested Molly.

"Listen to your father, sweetie," said Mom.

"But, Mom, this is *important*."

"I'm sure it's not a matter of life or death," said Dad.

"Well, then you're sure *wrong*," said Molly, getting increasingly annoyed.

"Molly, this is not a discussion," said Mom, firmly now. "This is supposed to be a nice family Christmas. After everything that's happened this year, I just wanted us to celebrate the fact we're all still together . . . and even have some new additions."

"Hyurgh!" said Dyandra.

Mr. Bones quietly took a sip of mulled wine, politely ignoring the argument.

Molly sighed. It wasn't like she, Grace, and Marty would be able to do much planning anyway. And maybe she could even talk to Mr. Bones about any potential curse antidotes, or at least more portable protections that were less stinky than garlic and more easily available year-round than mistletoe. Defeated, she ran upstairs and left her phone in her room, texting Grace she wouldn't be available before she left.

Christmas dinner with the Dades was as weird as always. (Well, maybe a *bit* weirder than last year.) Mom's gingerbread graveyard was still the centerpiece, though now half the gravestones were illegible as Molly was in charge of the physical side of things. Then there was stuffing using Grammy Dade's recipe, and red cabbage and Parmesan sweet potatoes as per usual. And everyone talked over one another without listening, just like every year.

But as everyone ate, talked, and groaned noisily, Molly found herself too distracted for conversation. Mr. Bones was unfortunately seated on the other side of the table, too far for Molly to pick his brain about how best not to die. Not even watching Dyandra demolish, very literally, several mince pies could rouse her, even though it left everyone else in stitches. Across the table, she felt her mom watching her, looking worried.

After what seemed much longer than usual, Christmas dinner was finally over. Everyone moved into the living room to gather around the fire, sleep off eating their own body weight in turkey, and in one case climb the Christmas tree screaming, "Merrr crusma!!"

Throughout it all Molly avoided her mother, who was hovering like she wanted to talk to her. After everything that had happened, Molly definitely did not want to talk. It was bad enough having to deal with a murderous witch classmate without having a parent dismiss it, *and* insist she put her phone away.

As a way of avoiding Mom, and also finding out if there was any way she wasn't completely doomed, Molly finally managed to corner Mr. Bones. "I am not aware of any cases of witch bottles getting jinxed," he said after she explained everything that had happened at the beach. "But based on what you are telling me about this Cara classmate staring at you, it sounds like she might have given you the Evil Eye."

"Okay, so how do I un–Evil Eye myself?" said Molly.

"Well, I've heard of people carrying various talismans

and amulets, and also rue, as protection," said Mr. Bones. "But I'd have to consult some grimoires—spell books in everyday English—if we're talking curse reversal."

"Do you have any . . . grimoires?" said Molly.

"Oh yes, several," said Mr. Bones, brushing mince pie crumbs off the knitted elf on his chest. "They make for very good bedtime reading. I'll get them out when I get home and see what I can find."

"Thanks, Mr. Bones," said Molly, suddenly aware of a ghostly form hovering behind her.

Mr. Bones noticed, too. "I'll . . . er, make myself scarce, shall I?" he said as he got up to leave. Molly shook her head desperately.

"Thank you," said Mom as she replaced him in the large wingback chair he had been sitting in. Molly groaned inwardly and folded her arms and hunched her shoulders outwardly. This was clearly not going to be a fun conversation.

"How are you feeling, sweetie?" said Mom. "You've been very quiet all day."

"Fine," said Molly.

"You sure?" said Mom, frowning. "I know I've been pretty distracted recently, what with Christmas, and home-schooling Dyandra, and letting people know we're a partly dead family. But I want you to know that I am here for you if you ever want to talk. About anything."

"Sure," said Molly.

"I know you and Marty are mad that I and Dad don't believe that whole curses and witches thing. I get it. But your father and I just want to—"

"Actually, Mom, I've been feeling really tired," said Molly. "I think I might be getting a headache. Can I go lie down?"

"Yes, of course," said Mom, seeming disappointed. Molly was getting used to that expression on adults. "Let us know if you need anything, okay?"

"Sure thing," said Molly, no longer able to look at her mother. She fled upstairs.

After checking that Greebo the dead cat was still under there, Molly flopped onto her bed. The boil felt worse, and she genuinely *was* starting to get a headache. At least all the stress from Cara cursing her had taken her mind off the fact that this was the first Christmas she'd spent with half her family dead. Which her mind was now back on. She needed a distraction.

Her phone sat on the bedside table showing several texts from Grace. Yawning, Molly went to check . . . and that's when she saw them. Sitting right there with all the normal messages. Sent today at 2:34 p.m.

Molly gasped and sat up, the pins and needles returning to every part of her body.

Cara Hartman had texted her.

Chapter
Twenty-One

◈

"**M**ARTY!!!" yelled Molly, eyes still on her phone. "CAN YOU COME UPSTAIRS?"

She must have sounded worried, because Marty got there quicker than normal. Seeing as normal was poltergeist speed for Marty, that was very fast indeed.

Molly held up her phone. "Look at this!"

"What the . . ." said Marty as he read Cara's messages:

Hey, I need to meet with you, privately.

Where we can't be seen.

The sea cave north of town okay?

No weird stuff.

"This has to be a trap, right?" said Marty once he'd finished.

"Right?!" said Molly, taking a screenshot of Cara's messages and texting it to Grace. "Definitely a trap. So I can't go . . . right?"

"Right," said Marty. "Although . . . can't she probably get in the house anyway? And the crematorium if she has the keys."

"Well, we don't *know* if it was her who got into the house that night," said Molly. "But, maybe? Why?"

"I dunno, that she can still get to you anyway?" said Marty. "I guess I'm just saying that ignoring a witch who maybe wants to kill you . . . might make the witch want to kill you *even more*."

"Yes, but I don't want to make it any easier for her to kill me either!" said Molly. "What should I do?!"

They both jumped as Molly's phone started ringing. Fortunately, it was only Grace. Molly turned the camera on to show her the boil.

"Oh wow, that looks painful," said Grace, wincing. "Have you grown any more boils?"

"Not yet," said Molly grimly.

Marty posted a message to the call: More importantly, what does Molly do about Cara? Does she meet her? Does she say no and maybe go into hiding?

Grace hesitated. "I think that maybe you shouldn't do anything to rile Cara up anymore. And if you agree to meet her, then at least you can see her coming and prepare yourself. And I dunno, maybe she can be reasoned with?"

"You remember what Ethan and Dee said about witches," said Molly grimly. "They're more into 'Death to my enemies' than hugging it out. But I guess you guys are right. I do need to meet her. If I don't, I'll just be watching over my shoulder for her anyway."

"Well, you won't need to go alone. I'm coming with you," said Grace firmly, proving once again she was the best friend in the whole world. Molly doubted that many other girls would accompany their friend to face down a murderwitch.

"Thanks, Grace," she said, sniffling.

"I'm coming, too, Moll," said Marty. "It's kinda my identity now to be the only ghost Dade sibling, and I don't want any competition."

"Thanks, you idiot," said Molly, now getting completely choked up.

"I can't hear what Marty said, but I'm sure it was really sweet," said Grace.

"Marty says he's coming, too," said Molly, rubbing her eyes self-consciously. "So I guess now I just need to respond to Cara."

It took Molly, Marty, and Grace collectively an hour and

a half to compose the messages Molly eventually sent. First, they debated whether to tell Cara that Marty and Grace were coming, or surprise her with Marty and Grace, before finally settling on telling her about Grace but not Marty since he was invisible. Then they went back and forth on whether to ask Cara to meet in a few days so they'd have time to prepare, or to meet tomorrow so Cara would have less time to kill Molly in her sleep (or at least add more boils). After that, they had to work out how to say this to Cara without incurring further witchy wrath. They finally settled on:

> Sure!
>
> Let's meet tomorrow at 1 pm—sound okay?
>
> Also, can I bring Grace?

And then they waited. Molly started biting her fingernails, which wasn't even a habit she had. Marty started pace-floating around the room. Grace stayed on the line and gave various theories as to why they hadn't heard back from Cara yet. These included Cara being busy sacrificing animals, some other kind of dark anti-Christmas ritual, and being away from her phone. Waiting for someone to message you back is stressful enough, even when you aren't concerned they are trying to kill you.

Molly even checked her email out of desperation, in case Cara somehow decided to contact her there. She had not, but there was something new. Dee Weston had replied to her message.

Molly!

Was great seeing you the other day, and really great to receive your email (though I guess we covered everything you asked in person when we bumped into each other, lol).

Anyway, I know this might seem out of the blue, but Ethan and I have found something we think you should see. It concerns your family.

We were working on our Roehampton episode, and we spotted something in the footage. We don't want to send it via email, because we aren't sure who is monitoring it (call me paranoid, but when you're in our line of work, it always pays to be safe!).

We'll be passing back near Roehampton tomorrow, if you are around to go over some recordings with us. I think your dad and brother might want to see this, too.

Anyway, let me know. Based on Google Maps, we should be there around 4–5 pmish. If not, then we can maybe meet up the next time we're in the area? (Which is a lot. New England be spooky.)

Thanks, and hopefully speak to you soon!

Dee

"What do you think?" said Molly after showing it to the others.

I think it sounds like they caught some footage of Mom, which is going to take some explaining, **messaged Marty on Grace's call.**

Also, what is up with everyone wanting to meet but
  not saying why?
Though I guess it's a good thing they're in town, right?
Maybe they could give us some advice.
If we survive our meeting with Cara.

"True," said Molly. "I think we might need to come clean with them about everything that's been going on. At this point we will need all the help we can get."

Good idea, **messaged Marty.** But maybe don't put anything in writing.

"Right. Good call," said Molly as she quickly typed a response and hit send.

"It's a shame they aren't coming *before* our meeting with Cara." Grace sighed. "That's if she ever respon—"

She was cut off by Molly's phone buzzing.

"It . . . it's Cara," said Molly. "She's replying!"

"And?" said Grace. "What does it say?"

Molly and Marty didn't respond, but instead just stared in shock at Molly's phone.

"Guys?" said Grace. "Guys?!"

Molly blinked and shook her head. "Sorry, Grace. It's just . . . you know what, I'll send you the screenshot."

When Grace read the messages, she gasped. "But, but . . . how does she *know*?"

Molly reread Cara's texts, just to make sure she wasn't in one of her nightmares. The pins and needles were very much back.

Yes, definitely bring Grace. I want witnesses this time.

Tomorrow, 1 pm is fine.

Bring Marty, too.

Chapter
Twenty-Two

It was the day after Christmas, the anniversary of Marty's and Mom's deaths. Under different circumstances, Molly might have spent the day brooding in her bedroom. Instead, she was riding her bike farther than she was officially allowed, with Marty perched behind her and Grace cycling by her side. In a weird way it was almost better, even if Molly was potentially pedaling toward her doom.

The sea cave entrance lay on the same stretch of rock that Roehampton Lighthouse was built on, but on the side facing away from town. The side that usually didn't get taken in photos, as Roehampton blocked the way of the glorious

Maine coastline. Molly and Grace pulled up and dumped their bikes.

Already there, propped neatly against a rock and securely locked, was another bike. It was the expensive kind and didn't have a single dent or scratch on it. Cara was here.

Molly turned on her flashlight and looked around the cave, Grace and Marty standing on either side of her. Slowly, they creeped in. The sides of the cave were covered with something slimy, and the air smelled damp and rotten.

"Isn't this cave supposed to be haunted?" said Grace, clutching Molly's arm.

"They say that about everywhere in Roehampton," said Molly, trying to sound braver than she felt. The ghosts were meant to be pirates, or smugglers, or something similarly criminal and seafaring—the stories varied. As far as Molly was concerned, they were the least frightening thing waiting for them in the cave that day. "Hello?" she called out, her voice echoing into the abyss.

"Back here!" said Cara's voice from deep within the cave. Molly shone her flashlight into the darkness. She couldn't see anything, but tiny squeaks rang out in the air above their heads.

Molly, Marty, and Grace tiptoed forward, ducking as the suspicious squeaking and fluttering noises continued above them. "Cara?" called out Molly again. "Where are you?"

"There aren't bats in here, are there?" asked Grace.

"Keep going," said Cara's voice, now sounding irritated. "And it's a *cave*, Grace. Of course there are bats."

Molly took a deep breath. She was beginning to doubt the wisdom of their plan. They were just two ordinary kids and a former ordinary kid turned poltergeist. What could they do against a witch who could control the weather, give the Evil Eye, and was potentially in league with the woman who cursed their house?

Against her better judgment, Molly edged farther into the cave, Marty and Grace both now clinging on to each arm. They were truly out of their depth now. The entrance lay worryingly far behind them, a smaller and smaller point of light in the gloom. What were they thinking? This was it. Death was going to take her on extremely neat wings in the form of prim and proper Cara Hartman.

Suddenly Molly's flashlight picked up on something small and dark. Her breath caught, and she swung the light back to reveal . . . some clothes folded tidily in a pile on a rock. A pristine pair of sneakers sat next to them. Cara's clothes . . . but no Cara.

"I'm behind the rock," called out Cara's voice. Molly looked at Grace, then looked at Marty (sort of), and took a deep breath, feeling a little better. If this *was* it, she wasn't going alone.

They rounded the rock. Molly swung her torch about, confused. There was still no sign of Cara.

"Down here," said Cara's voice. Molly lowered the flashlight. Looking up at her with big dark eyes was not Cara, but a small gray seal.

"It's me," said the seal in Cara's voice.

Molly, Marty, and Grace screamed, and Molly dropped the flashlight. Cara the seal sighed.

"Yeah, I figured you'd be more likely to believe me if you could see me," she said. "Surprise. I'm a selkie."

"A what now?" said Marty.

"A selkie," said Cara, rolling her seal eyes. "It's basically like a Scottish were-seal. All the women on my mom's side are."

"Oh. Cool," said Marty. "Wait—*you can hear me*?"

"Good catch," said Cara.

"Have you . . . *always* been able to hear Marty?" said Molly, nervously casting her mind back to all the things Marty had said behind Cara's back in class. Now she would definitely want to kill them.

"No," said Cara as Molly repressed a sigh of relief. "That's the other reason I met you in seal form. Well, that and I hoped you would be less likely to try anything if I looked like a cute little seal. I don't know if you noticed, but animals and babies can see and hear ghosts."

"We have," said Molly.

"Well, I'm an animal right now," said Cara, raising a flipper to make her point.

"How often does this happen?" said Grace.

"I can change forms whenever I want. That's the nice thing about being a selkie, no need to wait for full moons or anything like that," said Cara. "I'm a seal pretty regularly. Swimming is my main form of exercise, and the Atlantic feels much better with fur."

"I bet," said Grace.

"I actually once considered becoming a seal full-time," continued Cara, "but Mom said I had to go to school."

"So . . . you brought us out here to tell us you're a seal sometimes?" said Marty.

"No, Marty, I brought you out here to tell you something I *heard* when I was a seal," said Cara. "You'd be amazed what you can find out when people see you as part of the coastline. That's how I found out about what's going on with your family. I was there that day at the beach when Molly told Grace everything."

Molly desperately tried to remember if she had said anything mean about Cara in that conversation. Was that what this was all about?

"But that part doesn't matter," Cara continued, as Molly repressed her second sigh of relief of the day. "The more important point is what I heard your creepy older friends talking about. The ones with all the fancy recording equipment. I saw you talking to them on a different day."

"Ethan and Dee?" said Molly, now completely confused. "What about them?"

"Well, after you left, they kept talking. About their plans to hunt you down," said Cara. "They are *not* your friends."

The dizziness had returned. The pins and needles would be coming any second. "What?" said Molly.

"They're monster hunters! They were in Roehampton because they are out to get you and your family," said Cara. "I heard *everything.* They've been trailing you since they got here! And they only left town to get supplies in order to rig your dad's new crematorium. They're going to blow it up!"

The pieces had already begun to fall together in Molly's mind, but the picture they formed when linked together was too frightening for her to believe. The pins and needles started pricking her hands with a vengeance.

"They're planning to stage another accident to take you out—just like they did last year!" continued Cara. "That explosion that killed you, Marty, was *not* an accident."

Chapter
Twenty-Three

∞

Silence descended on the cave. Molly was the first to break it. "Okay, saying this is all true," she said, rubbing her temples. "Why us? Why the Dades?"

Everyone stared at her.

"Okay, I mean apart from the obvious. But Ethan and Dee don't know that, do they?" said Molly. "And what about last year—we were all still alive then."

Cara shrugged. "Well, I don't know if they've worked out that your sister is a zombie or that Marty and your mom are still hanging around," she said, "so I don't know if they have an exorcism planned, or anything like that. But they *definitely* know you're a witch."

Molly tried to speak in protest, but her mouth failed her. Anger joined the confusion and terror dancing around her brain.

Cara continued, "They spent a long time talking about all the signs a witch was in town, just like there were before they killed your mom and Marty last year. Storms, dead animals, things like that? That's *why* they blew up your mom's art studio, because they thought your mom was a witch, too."

"Whoa . . ." said Marty, his voice slightly choked.

"And that's why they decided to come back to Roehampton, because the weird stuff still kept happening. They were wondering if you knew that they were onto you being a witch, Molly," added Cara. "Which I guess you weren't if you're this shocked."

"But . . . but . . . *I'm* not a witch!" Molly finally managed to splutter. "You are!"

"No, I'm a selkie," said Cara. Molly had never seen a seal look annoyed before. It was unnerving. "Look, I don't need to do this. Not after you threw all those chairs and desks at me."

"You threw them at *me*!" said Molly, outraged.

"No, *you* threw them at *me*," said Cara with exaggerated patience. "And then after you *literally flew out of the room*, I was stuck with a whole bunch of chairs and desks blocking the door. I had to spend nearly half an hour moving them so

I could get out. In the dark! Because you blew out the lights!"

"No, *you* did!" said Molly, gripping her flashlight and balling her other hand into a tight fist. The pins and needles were running up and down her body now.

"And that's not even including the stuff you pulled at the Christmas concert. You could have rehearsed—"

"I DID!" Molly's heart raced and her stomach was doing flips. Her flashlight started to flicker.

"Mr. Anderson was counting on you," said Cara. "And instead you blew it, and then when I tried to fix your mess, you blew it for everyone else, too! By throwing a piano!"

"That was *you*!" said Molly, feeling increasingly light-headed and dizzy. The pins and needles pooled in Molly's fingers and toes, feeling like tiny electric shocks.

"Mr. Anderson was basically in tears over that email from the superintendent," added Cara.

"SHUT UP!" yelled Molly, dropping her flashlight as her hands spasmed open.

To her surprise Cara did shut up and stared at her, seal mouth open in shock. Grace and Marty were also staring at her. Molly looked down. The pins and needles didn't just *feel* like electric shocks. Actual sparks were flying from her fingers.

Molly held up her hands. What looked like tiny bolts of lightning were dancing around them, crackling and sparking, before dying down like fireworks fading in the sky. She kept staring at them, barely able to believe what she had just seen.

"You were saying?" said Cara.

"OMG," said Grace. "Molly! You're not cursed by a witch! You *are* a witch!"

Molly shook her head, still stunned. "But, but . . . what about the boil on my chin?"

"I think maybe that actually *is* a zit," said Marty.

Molly stared at him while Cara seal-smirked.

"What did Marty say?" asked Grace.

"Don't—" said Molly as Grace's phone beeped.

"Oh . . ." said Grace after she read Marty's message, looking at Molly guiltily.

"So if I believe *you*," Cara narrowed her large brown eyes, "and you weren't aware you were a witch until just now . . . then what was that weird stuff with the bottles at the beach the other day?"

"That was meant to be protection from y— Oh, never mind," said Molly, shamefacedly.

"What were *you* doing there?" said Marty.

"I'd just finished my morning swim! I had just changed back into human form and was about to go home when I spotted you doing weird stuff with seawater and herbs. You get how that looked like witchcraft, right?"

"Okay, but that was *anti*-witchcraft, not actual witchcraft," admitted Molly finally. "I'd been feeling all these symptoms, and Ethan and Dee said that they were signs of being cursed by a witch. And after all the weird stuff that had been happening, I assumed that I *was*. I didn't realize they were all signs of me having secret witch powers!" She felt the zit-not-boil on her chin throb. "And, uh, puberty I guess."

"You . . . you really didn't know?" said Cara, shaking her smooth gray head. "You threw a piano with your mind, and chairs and desks . . . and you didn't know you were doing it?" She seal-barked with laughter.

"It's not *that* funny," said Molly, glowering down at Cara. She didn't have any right to look so cute and seal-like while actively mocking her.

"You know, we *are* descended from someone who was accused of witchcraft at the trials . . ." said Marty, Grace's phone beeping as he filled her in electronically. "This actually makes a lot of sense."

"Oh man, after the desks, when I saw you doing that weird stuff at the beach, I assumed that you were going full wicked witch and were assembling a coven with Grace or something!" said Cara, still laughing.

"Ohhh, so that's why you were staring at us like that," said Marty. "Like you were mad. We thought you were trying to give us the Evil Eye."

"How could I do that by just staring at you angrily? You

know that's not possible, Marty," said Cara as Molly and Marty looked at each other. "Anyway, I actually thought those bottles you were making were maybe *you* trying to curse *me*. Or at least scare me—don't think I didn't notice the wind picking up when you spotted me."

"Again, that was an accident. I didn't realize I was doing it," said Molly. "I think, in hindsight, my powers come out when I'm stressed. Or maybe that's when I can't control them. I mean, we really did think *you* were trying to curse *us*—I'd say that's pretty stressful!"

"Hence the wind!" said Grace, hands on her mouth. "Wait, and the chairs and the desks, and the Christmas concert! You were really upset!"

"And when Timothy was messing up the big game last year," said Marty as Grace's phone beeped. "Remember the frogs?"

"Oh wow, I forgot all about the frogs," said Molly. She looked down at Cara, who was still making a very un-seal-like smirk. Something suddenly occurred to her. "Wait, if you thought I was trying to curse you, or at least scare you, then why did you try to warn me about Ethan and Dee?"

"After the chairs and desks, I nearly didn't," admitted Cara. "But then when I saw you at the beach, I don't know, even though I thought you were doing creepy witch stuff, it reminded me that you are a person. Like a modern-day

Goody Proxmire, still getting hunted. And I may not like you, and you may have thrown desks and a piano at me, okay, by accident, whatever. But that doesn't mean I want you to *die*."

"Oh man, Cara, I am *so* sorry we had you all wrong," said Molly, now feeling incredibly guilty. "You are a really good person." She paused for a moment. "Or, uh, a really good seal."

"Both." Cara shrugged.

"I'm sorry, too," said Grace, nodding emphatically.

"Me too," said Marty. "But also, we should go home and warn everyone RIGHT NOW. Ethan and Dee will be at our place soon, remember?"

"What?!" said Cara, the little whiskers that made her seal eyebrows raised.

"We . . . uh . . . kinda invited the Westons to our house when we didn't know they were trying to kill us," said Molly. "So they could be arriving any moment."

"Okay, I'm coming with you," said Cara firmly. "Your family will be more likely to believe you that way. I'll even change into a seal if I have to."

"Cara, thank you so much," said Molly. "Again, I'm so sorry we thought you were—"

"Oh, whatever," said Cara. "You should all turn around, I need to turn back into a human if I'm going to ride my bike." Her seal eyes turned serious. "Trust me, you don't want to see this. It involves turning my skin inside out."

Chapter
Twenty-Four

Molly, Marty, and Grace obediently turned their backs. There was a series of horrible squelching and slurping noises behind them that seemed to go on forever.

"Hey, sorry, Cara, do you think you could speed this up?" said Marty as he craned his neck around. "The rest of our family's at home, and seeing as we have monster hunters coming for us we— AAAAAARGH!" Molly sensed her brother's head snap back to face the front, eyes wide with horror.

"I *told* you transforming involved turning my skin inside out," said Cara's voice from behind them. "What did you *think* it was going to look like?"

"I don't know?! Not that!" said Marty. "It was so much worse than I was expecting! *So much worse!*"

Cara and Molly sighed simultaneously.

"What did Marty say?" said Grace. Her phone beeped.

Molly shifted on her feet from side to side as the squelching continued. This felt awkward. "I really am sorry, Cara," she said, looking up at the cave ceiling. Several pairs of small beady eyes blinked back at her, so she looked back down. "You are actually a much better person than me. Thank you so much again for warning us."

"I know, and it's okay," said Cara. "I actually feel pretty guilty it took me so long to tell you—I felt terrible yesterday until I made my decision. I guess I was mad. Because I thought you'd progressed to cursing me, and you were always mean to me before that."

"I thought that you were being mean to *me*," said Molly, feeling ashamed as several memories flashed through her mind. "I guess I thought I was defending myself or something. But you're right, I have been mean."

"I've been mean, too," admitted Cara. "I get frustrated, because I always have to work so hard, and *really* try. And then you just come in with your cool clothes knowing you look awesome, and then you *beat* me without any effort, knowing you can."

"You think my clothes are cool?" said Molly in wonder.

"Also, Molly *really* tries. You should have heard her practicing for the Christmas concert," said Marty. "I heard 'God Rest Ye Merry Gentlemen' so many times I nearly died again."

"He's right. I *do* try. All the time," said Molly. "I don't ever walk around thinking I look great or that I'm going to win at anything. Like ever."

"I'm too much of a human to hear Marty now," said Cara. "But I think I get the gist."

The unearthly squelches had finally stopped. After a brief pause, Cara called out, "Okay, you can turn around now."

There stood Cara all right, fully dressed, and still somehow perfectly immaculate and unruffled. Her hair was tied back neatly as always, as sleek and shiny as her seal fur. She did not look at all like she had gotten dressed in a cave immediately after a gruesome transformation.

"How . . . how do you *do* that?" said Molly.

"Do what?" said Cara, looking at Molly like she was speaking in tongues. "Anyway, don't we need to get going?"

"Right!"

The kids ran out of the cave and onto their bikes. Snow started falling gently halfway on their ride home, the first of this winter.

"Of course it's snowing now," said Molly. "Of course."

"It would be great if you learned how to turn it off one day," said Marty. "Seeing as you can control the wind apparently."

The ride into Roehampton seemed to take even longer than the ride out. The cold air hurt Molly's throat and chest, but she pedaled as fast as she could. Little sparks flew out of her fingers, streaming behind her as she willed herself to go faster.

"Careful!" Grace yelled out behind her, dodging the sparks.

"I'm sorry, I really don't know how to control this!" said Molly.

The sparks continued flying as the houses they passed grew closer and closer together. "While this isn't exactly helping us not stand out, I have to admit this looks pretty cool," said Marty.

Molly laughed, which made the pins and needles recede. The sparks died down.

They were in Roehampton proper now, speeding past the quaint cafés still decked out for Christmas and tourist stores filled with lobster, lighthouse, and Goody Proxmire merchandise. They passed Grace's dads' B-and-B, rounded a corner, and in Molly's case nearly skidded off her bike. Her stomach flipped, and the wind picked up.

"Not now, not now," she muttered as she righted herself,

Marty gripping her shoulders invisibly. Ahead of them lay the old wrought-iron cemetery gates. They were nearly home.

Once inside the graveyard, Molly and Grace jumped off, threw their bikes and helmets down on the ground, and made to sprint. Meanwhile, Cara dismounted, removed her helmet, propped her bike up neatly against the wall, and was about to start locking it up when she saw Molly and Grace staring at her.

"Cara, we literally don't have any time!" said Molly desperately. "We need to find my family right NOW— Oh *hi*, Mr. Anderson!" Molly fixed a polite smile to hide any panic on her face.

"Hi, Molly; hi, Cara; hi, Grace!" said Mr. Anderson, who had just walked past them carrying five bunches of carnations. He looked somewhat less morose than when they last saw him, which admittedly wasn't saying much. "Good seeing you all. I was just paying my annual Christmas visit to my mom and dad. And my brother. And both my sisters." He looked down at his flowers before smiling sympathetically at Molly. "I lost a couple of them around this time of year. Though I suppose you know all about that, Molly."

Molly was concerned that she was going to know even more about that if she didn't find her parents soon. "Yeah . . . uh . . . you haven't seen my par—my *dad* around today, have you? Or my brother?"

"Oh yes, just now in fact!" said Mr. Anderson. Molly sighed with relief. "They were with a young couple wearing some very trendy outfits."

Molly was no longer relieved. "Was the woman wearing a leather jacket?" she said.

"That's right!" said Mr. Anderson.

"Oh! Okay!" said Molly, feeling the pins and needles in her fingers again. The wind picked up. Cara and Grace looked at each other. "Um, you didn't see where they went, did you?"

"No, sorry. I was thinking too much about death at the time," said Mr. Anderson. "Wasn't paying much attention to my surroundings."

"Hmmm!" said Molly in an attempt to not scream in frustration, and feeling very guilty about this. "Okay . . . well, thanks, Mr. Anderson. But, uh . . . we need to get going. Right now."

"Sure thing. Merry belated Christmas!" said Mr. Anderson.

"Merry belated Christmas!" called out Molly, Grace, Cara, and (unheard by Mr. Anderson) Marty. They were already running to the Dades' house.

When they got there, the back door was open.

"Oh no!" said Grace.

"Okay, let's head in quietly," said Molly. "Maybe we can get the jump on them."

They tiptoed, and in one case floated, as quietly as they could into the house. The kitchen was deserted, a half-empty cup of coffee and another half-empty cup of tea on the table. A pile of old leather books covered in weird symbols sat next to the tea. Molly grabbed a knife from the knife block on the counter and edged her way farther in.

There was a note on the table next to the coffee, written in handwriting Molly did not recognize. She put down the kitchen knife and picked up the piece of paper.

Molly Dade,

We have your family. Meet us in the crematorium when you find this message, and they may still live.

We know who and what you are, and what you have done. We have dealt with your kind before. We have come prepared for you.

Do not expect to escape us, witch.

"Ohhh . . ." said Marty. "Oh, this is not good."

Chapter
Twenty-Five

∽

The pins and needles returned. Molly stumbled backward and was caught by Grace. Above them the lights flickered.

"Molly . . ." said Grace. "I know you must be really stressed right now. But please try not to blow out the lights or throw any furniture. We need to go rescue your family."

"Grace is right," said Cara, putting a firm hand on Molly's shoulder. "Come on, let's go!"

They ran. Out the kitchen, past Mom's old studio, past Josiah Moffit's grave. They sped out of the oldest part of the cemetery, through the Victorian section, and into the newest area, the graves going from rough slate to worn marble to shiny granite as they did.

They ran past Mr. Anderson again as he lay flowers on his family's tomb and waved to them. The snow was coming down harder now, sticking to their hair and coats. None of them felt the cold, fear powering them despite their exhaustion.

Finally, they reached the new crematorium. The door was open.

Molly stopped and turned to Grace and Cara. "You don't need to come in with me. This is between me and the Westons. I'm the only one they're after."

"Well, I'm coming anyway," said Cara. "I don't think I'd be able to live with myself if you died or something."

"I'm coming, too," said Grace. "You're my best friend, and I'm not letting you do this alone."

"I'm obviously coming," said Marty. "You're my sister, and it's not like they can kill me *again*."

"Guys . . ." said Molly, getting choked up again.

"Oh, whatever," said Cara, rolling her eyes. "We need to go in *now*. They have your family."

Molly nodded. She tiptoed in, Marty floating next to her. Grace and Cara followed. Feeling her way in the dark, Molly found the switch and turned on the light. It flashed and dimmed before gradually, slowly, illuminating the room. Molly looked around.

"There's no one here!" she said, looking around the enormous high-tech furnace for any possible hidden nook.

"You don't think . . . ?" said Grace, looking uneasily at the furnace. Molly's stomach dropped immediately, and the crematorium door slammed shut. Everyone yelped.

"Sorry, I think that was me," said Molly. "I . . . I don't want to check."

"I'll do it," said Cara, squaring her shoulders.

Molly covered her eyes. "Okay, you'll need to use the touch screen on the right to open it. Let me know if you need any help."

"It's okay," said Cara. There were a series of metallic clangs that sounded like the furnace doors. "This touch screen is actually really intuitive. Also, your family is not in the furnace, we're good."

Molly opened her eyes again. Meanwhile Marty slid himself into the machine. "I'm just checking to see if anything's changed since the other day, or been tampered with, or . . ." He paused just long enough to make Molly terrified. "Oh *no*."

"What is it?" said Molly, pressing her ear to the smooth enamel of the furnace. Dad had fixed the scratch already. She turned back to Grace and Cara, who were looking increasingly alarmed. "Marty's looking to see if Ethan and Dee messed with the machinery. Then he said, 'Oh no.' And now I'm freaking out."

"I said 'Oh no' because we are in serious trouble," said Marty. "They've been really smart about this. They've messed with it, but not with explosives, with just a small amount of extra stuff that will overload this whole machine and cause it to blow once they turn the furnace on." He shook his head. "I guess they were concerned that another random explosion would look suspicious. This way, if anyone investigates properly, they won't find anything they weren't expecting, and will just assume that the furnace blew up due to a malfunction."

"Marty says that they've rigged the machine to blow up once it's turned on so it looks like an accident," said Molly to Cara and Grace.

"Which everyone in town will buy because they believe in 'Goody Proxmire's curse'!" said Grace, her hands at her mouth.

"Exactly," said Molly. "Everyone's practically *expecting* something to happen to us again. It's the perfect cover."

"It *is* the perfect cover," said a familiar voice behind them. Molly, Grace, Cara, and Marty slowly turned around. The main door was open, and in it stood Ethan and Dee Weston. They had Dad and Timothy tied up in front of them. Ethan held a bejeweled gold dagger to Dad's neck, and Dee held a black, ancient-looking blade to Timothy's. Already inside the crematorium were Mr. Bones and Dyandra, also tied up.

Mom hovered behind them, looking helpless. Fortunately, the Westons didn't seem to realize she was there. She looked at Molly and shook her head desperately.

"We *did* tell you we'd be coming back," said Ethan, his eyes glittering with a hatred Molly had never seen before.

"I didn't think it would be so soon," said Molly, glancing nervously back at Mom.

Dee snorted. "Oh, you thought you were so clever, didn't you? Playing the cute little skeptic kid with us. I bet you thought you had us fooled."

"Well, I wasn't exactly playing . . ." said Molly.

"Don't try. We saw right through you from the start, from that first day we met you. And this time we came prepared," said Dee.

"I'm holding the sacred knife of St. Cuthbert, and Dee here has the legendary obsidian blade of Constantinople," said Ethan. "Both of which offer us plenty of protection against your dark magic."

"I'm somewhat of an expert in these things, and I have heard of neither," interrupted Mr. Bones. "And I do think I would have, if they were as legendary as you claim. Whoever sold you those was having you on. I hope you didn't pay too much."

"SILENCE!" said Ethan. "We can see that they work. Look at how the demon child is trembling. Her powers have no effect against these most sacred and holy of objects!"

"I'm honestly more worried about how sharp they are, and that they are pointed at my dad and brother," said Molly.

"Then they work!" said Ethan triumphantly.

"And if you don't want us to use them on your family, I suggest you tie up your little friends. Right now," said Dee, tossing Molly a length of rope with her free hand. "We hate to leave loose ends . . . and any associate of a witch is not to be trusted."

Marty whispered in Molly's ear. "Try to stall them, Moll. I'll see if I can do anything to stop this machine from blowing up."

Molly nodded. She slowly walked behind Grace and began tying her hands together, taking her time. "So . . . you must have had this planned for a long time, huh?"

"Hurry up!" said Ethan.

"Sure thing," said Molly, speeding up as slowly as she dared. "So how did you find out about me? I mean, I only just found out myself, so you guys must be *really* good." *There is no way they are going to fall for this*, she thought.

"We *are* good. The best." Dee smirked. "We come from a long line of exorcists and monster hunters."

Molly had finished Grace's ties, and moved on to Cara as slowly as she dared. "Ouch!" yelped Cara.

"That doesn't surprise me," said Molly, ignoring Cara

and trying to sound suitably fearful and impressed. At least she didn't have to fake the fearful part.

"Our own mother was killed by a witch in the line of duty when we were twelve," added Ethan.

"Was . . . was she trying to kill the witch at the time?" said Molly. She had nearly finished with Cara's ties now and quietly started to slow down, hoping the Westons were distracted enough not to notice.

"What does that matter?" snapped Dee.

Mr. Bones coughed. "Well . . . rather a lot in the court of law, I'm afraid. It's the difference between premeditated murder and self-defense."

"We didn't ask you!" said Ethan, snarling.

"Sorry," said Mr. Bones.

Marty popped out of the furnace and whispered again in Molly's ear. "Keep going. If they turn this on before I find a way to disable their doomsday device, I won't be able to stop it. I hate to admit it, but they *are* good."

Fortunately, the Westons seemed to be on a roll. Molly tried cringing a little, hoping it would encourage them to taunt her more. She'd finished with the knots that bound Cara's wrists, but she moved her hands as if she were still going, hoping the distraction held.

"We are *proud* to continue Mom's legacy," said Dee. "The podcast gives us the perfect excuse. We travel around the country, pretend to investigate, record a few things. Then once that's done, BAM! We take out whatever we find on our actual investigation. Send them back to hell."

"We've killed vampires, werewolves, zombies," said Ethan.

"BYAAAAARGH!" said Dyandra.

"Bigfoots, selkies," added Dee, nodding. Cara glared at her, her large eyes furious and her lips a thin tight line. Dee did not seem to notice.

"Mothmen, mothwomen," continued Ethan. "But once a year, at Christmastime, in honor of our mom"—he bent down so that he was face-to-face with Molly—"we go on a *witch hunt*."

"I see you have finished tying up your friends," said Dee. Molly's hands began to shake. "Come here and turn around."

Molly complied, and desperately tried to think of something else that would distract them. The pins and needles were running up and down her arms and hands. Maybe she could channel them into sparks again and then use that to escape. Somehow. While saving everyone from the imminent explosion at the same time.

She heard the sound of Marty groaning from within the furnace. Her stomach started to drop, she felt dizzy, but no sparks came out.

"*Oh NO!*" said Marty.

Chapter Twenty-Six

Molly tried not to look in the direction of the furnace, but that didn't sound good. They needed more time; what was left to distract Ethan and Dee? She had to think of something that would keep them talking, and soon. Preferably something that would make them so sidetracked they wouldn't notice the time.

Like how Mom got when talking about art or baking, or how Timothy was when chatting basketball, or Dad with regard to anything to do with his furnace. Molly just needed to get the Westons talking about whatever their "thing" was.

The ornate gold knife glittered against her dad's neck.

Ethan and Dee's thing was pretty obvious from where she was standing. Hunting and killing people like her and her family.

"Well, seeing as how I'm about to die—" said Molly, as Mom made a clearly audible involuntary sob. Ethan and Dee looked around, confused. This was the wrong sort of distraction, the kind that could lead them to stabbing Dad and Timothy.

Molly tried again. "Seeing as how I'm about to die," she repeated firmly as the Westons turned back around, "could you at least tell me how you found me? I never told anyone until today, so I don't understand how you did it."

Dee took her obsidian blade away from Timothy's throat and stuck it in a scabbard clipped onto her vintage jeans. She walked over to Molly, clutching a rope, while Ethan kept his knife on Dad.

"We've been scoping out Roehampton for some time now." Dee smirked. "Between its history and the weird things that keep happening, we *knew* there had to be something sinister here."

"Showers of frogs at the basketball game, the lighthouse turning on by itself. Things that spoke to a dark presence," said Ethan.

"Given the town's past, we knew that this had to be the work of a witch!" said Dee. "We searched the family trees of Roehampton, looking for any descendants of

Goody Proxmire and her original coven that still lived in town." She tightened the ropes around Molly's wrists. Molly winced, said nothing, and hoped they'd keep talking.

"Then we visited Roehampton last Christmas for our annual witch hunt," said Ethan. "We scoped out the descendants we found in our research and found your dear, late mother."

"We got your address online and looked in the windows of the old crematorium that she pretended was her studio. A place of *death*," said Dee. "And of course, we caught her right in the act! She was in the middle of some dark spell involving feathers, string, and seawater in ceramic containers."

"That just sounds like one of Mom's weird art installations," said Timothy.

"That's right! It wasn't anything occult!" whispered Mom. "That was just my latest piece, *The Rhythm of the Sea!*"

The Westons looked around again. Molly started coughing loudly.

"Sorry," she said as Ethan and Dee looked back at her, eyes narrowed. "Something in my throat."

Dee had finished tying Molly's hands together and was now tying something *to* them. Whatever it was jingled faintly. "We knew then that your mother must have been responsible for everything that was happening in Roehampton. She had to be stopped."

"So we broke in and set everything up with a timer for a little explosion," said Ethan.

"How could y—" said Dad before he was cut off by Ethan pressing the bright golden knife closer to his throat.

"And Marty?" said Molly, her voice low and angry.

Ethan shrugged. "That was unintentional. He just happened to be there, wrong place, wrong time." His knife was still at Dad's throat, but Molly saw her father's eyes bugging out in silent rage.

"Though if he was the son of a witch, it was only a matter of time before his evil tendencies began to show," said Dee, brushing back a strand of hair. It caused the sleeve of her leather jacket to ride up, exposing the geometric tattoo that Molly spotted that first day at the B-and-B. She hadn't recognized it at the time, but now she saw that it was . . .

"An apotropaic mark!" Molly gasped. "You're the ones who burned them into the auditorium ceiling! And carved the one onto the tree! And the one on Mom's old kiln! *And the one on the new furnace!*"

Dad's eyes bugged out more. Behind him, Ethan smiled. "Well done. You can never be too careful."

"Then we snagged the keys to the crematorium when one of you was kind enough to leave your back door open a few nights ago," said Dee. "It gave us plenty of time to set everything up in here without getting disturbed."

"I think that was me," said Timothy. "I was the last one in the house that night. Sorry, guys, my bad."

Under normal circumstances Molly would have yelled at Tim, but she needed to keep the Westons too occupied to remember to kill them. She kept her voice as mellow as she could. "So what brought you back? You'd already completed your mission." Molly craned around so she could keep her eyes on Ethan, his knife, and her dad.

Ethan grimaced. "After blowing up your mother, we went home. We assumed that it was all over. But then the reports from Roehampton didn't stop!"

"Instead they got *worse*," said Dee. "Strange groans from the graveyard. Headless squirrels and ducks. Unseasonal lightning. And that's when we realized that Momma Dade must have passed on the craft to her own wretched offspring."

"So we came back," said Ethan. "Imagine our luck when we met you on our first day. We started scoping you out. And what did we find?"

"You, throwing pianos with your mind!" said Dee. "Desecrating graves! Getting grimoires delivered to you by your creepy British friend just today!"

"Okay, but the piano wasn't on purpose! I didn't even realize I was doing it at the time!" said Molly. "And the grave thing was all a *big* misunderstanding—"

"Enough!" screeched Ethan, his voice getting increasingly hysterical. Dad gulped as the knife pressed even closer into his neck. "The point is, this child has engaged in unholy acts! She's made frogs rain down from ceilings! She's thrown inanimate objects at people! She's *raised the dead!*"

"Hurgh?" said Dyandra.

"Oh yes, don't think we haven't noticed that this little abomination DOESN'T HAVE A PULSE!" said Ethan. He finally took his knife away from Dad's throat to point in outrage at Dyandra with it. She stuck her tongue out at him.

"Oh, this is *fascinating!*" said Mr. Bones, suddenly very excited. Ethan and Dee turned and stared at him, their mouths slightly open. "Sorry to interrupt again, it's just that you saying 'raised the dead' made something occur to me. I wonder if, maybe, it was Molly's grief at losing her mother and brother that triggered her witch powers to go off in such a spectacular way. So spectacularly, in fact, that they brought everyone—erm—*Dyandra* back."

Molly gasped. She barely remembered anything about that terrible night, or what had happened in those lost hours in between Marty and Mom dying and returning. Her mind had blocked it out, and she was honestly glad about that. But now she tried to cast her mind back. . . . She could remember something from the morning after. Right before she saw Marty and Mom. Vague memories of sobbing into her pillow, and willing with every single fiber of her being for them to—

"OH," said Molly.

"Oh, sweetie! You managed to bring us back, and raise Dyandra from the grave?" whispered Mom into her ear, softly enough that the Westons thankfully didn't hear this time.

"Oh, Molly. I'm just so *proud* of you, pumpkin," said Dad, misty-eyed, which the Westons *did* hear. They turned and scowled at him, which Dad did not notice as he was getting too emotional.

"Molly, this is *so cool!*" said Timothy, grinning with the enthusiasm of someone who was not currently tied up and about to die. "You're an almost teenage witch!" His jaw dropped. "Wait! So it was you who saved us with the frogs at the big game last year?"

"I . . . think so?" said Molly.

"That is AWESOME!" he said, bouncing up and down despite his binds.

"Will you all just SHUT UP!" screamed Ethan, spittle flying in outrage. "She is an unclean wretch in league with the Evil One! Stop being so SUPPORTIVE."

"Oh, let's leave them, Ethan," said Dee, her voice eerily, icily calm. She was standing by the touch screen, finger poised. It was lit up, blinking in a way that Molly really hoped was Marty interfering. Her stomach dropped . . . but nothing happened.

Meanwhile, Dee tapped the screen. First firmly, and then with increasing fury. "Damned thing keeps on acting up . . ." she said, sounding a little less icily calm. Marty chuckled deep from within the furnace. Molly bit her lip and hoped he could hold it.

Dee tapped the screen again. It flashed, then changed screens. An ominous beeping sound filled the room. Molly heard Marty wail, "Noooo!"

"HA!" exclaimed Dee. The furnace started, shaking and clanking in a way that did not sound healthy. Molly flexed her fingers as much as she could with her hands tied together. Why weren't her powers working? What was wrong?

"As I was saying," said Dee, smiling triumphantly, "let's leave them, Ethan. This furnace will blow in a few minutes. They haven't got long for this world anyway."

"The Kremragende would *never* blow up!" said Dad, horrified. "It's the latest in Danish eco-technology! It won safety awards!"

"This Kremragende *will*," said Ethan as he opened the door. "We've made sure of it."

Dad gasped.

"And it's no using trying any of that witchcraft, Molly," added Dee as she followed her brother out. "You can't. You may have removed the mark we left on the furnace, but now . . . the whole floor is an apotropaic mark."

Chapter
Twenty-Seven

The door slammed shut.

Molly looked down. There, etched into the concrete floor, was indeed a giant apotropaic mark. It reached the walls and all the way over to the side of the furnace. The Westons were not kidding around.

"Oh, Molly, I'm so sorry," sobbed Mom. "And I'm so sorry, too, Marty."

"Me too. We should have believed you," said Dad.

"I just felt so terrible and guilty after the explosion. I thought it was all my fault," said Mom, her head bowed. "Which meant I couldn't bring myself to talk about it at all.

I should have dealt with that rather than dismiss you. I should have *listened* instead."

"I'm sorry, too, Molly and Marty," said Timothy. "After accusing Mr. Bones *and* Cara of being witches, I legit thought you'd lost it. It didn't occur to me that someone was actually after us. And also that witches are real, and you are one." Molly looked nervously over at Mr. Bones and Cara, who were politely ignoring the family drama along with Grace.

Marty emerged from the furnace. It clanked and rumbled threateningly, and the room was already getting oppressively hot. "Thanks, guys, I really appreciate this," he said. "But I'm trying to hold this machine together to keep it from blowing. And if I'm actually going to turn it off, I'll need some pliers, or some wire cutters, or something like that. Like RIGHT NOW." He ducked back in.

"Can't you, I dunno, hack into the system and break it?" said Molly.

"I *tried*, but this is surprisingly well-designed and hard to hack," said Marty, now from deep within the furnace.

"I knew it!" said Dad.

"The most I could do is mess with the touch screen a little," added Marty. "And even then, I couldn't do that for long."

"So what else can we do?" said Molly.

"Wire cutters!" Marty insisted. "This whole thing is

rigged so that the only way to stop it now is directly cutting off the power from within, physically!"

"Do you have anything sharp?" yelled Molly to Cara and Grace. They shook their heads.

"But, Marty, you can always work electronics!" said Timothy.

"Look, I can poltergeist-hack into things. Sending messages, uploading files, that stuff," said Marty, his voice straining. "But I can't cut things without physical tools. The most I can do right now is try to reduce the flow of electricity. I'm doing that right now . . . but I don't know how long I can hold it for."

"Okay, then does anyone have any keys so we can get out of here before it blows?" asked Molly.

Everyone shook their heads. "They emptied our pockets when they ambushed us," explained Dad.

"I'm trying to call 911," said Cara, contorting her body to punch the phone peeking out of her pocket desperately. "But there is literally no signal."

"There never has been in here," said Molly. "But keep trying!"

"I could go outside? I can walk through walls," suggested Mom. "We saw Mr. Anderson earlier, he might still be around. I could get him to raise the alarm!"

"Whoever he finds probably won't get here in time," said Marty. "I think I can do this for five more minutes, max!"

"Marty doesn't think that there's time," said Molly to Grace and Cara. "Also, couldn't Mom raising the alarm potentially expose us?" she said, turning back to her family.

"It's still worth a shot!" said Timothy. "It's better than dying! Or dying again!"

"Yerrrhh!" said Dyandra.

"Okay, we can try that if we can't think of anything else!" said Dad. "Molly, how about you try your magic to stop the machine? Or unlock the doors?"

Molly shook her head. "I can't do my magic. I tried . . . but I guess the apotropaic mark worked."

"But didn't you shut the door by accident earlier?" said Marty. Molly started. She'd forgotten about that in all the panic.

"Well," said Mr. Bones. "That mark is meant to ward against evil or harmful influences . . . not magic in general. So, er, are you evil?"

"I don't think so?" said Molly.

"Definitely not!" said Mom.

"Try dimming the lights or something," said Marty.

Molly closed her eyes, still doubtful. If stress caused her powers to break out, surely something should have happened by now? Unless that was just her choking. Her hands shook.

She concentrated on the feeling, of the waves of fear riding with the pins and needles shooting up and down her arms. If she could somehow let go of those doubts and move that feeling . . . above her. Above her and up.

Molly opened her eyes. The lights were flickering and blinking.

"You did it, Moll!" said Timothy. "This is all SO COOL."

"Oh, pumpkin," said Dad, now truly teary-eyed.

"There, you see!" said Mr. Bones. "The silly fools were daft enough to not tell the difference between good magic and bad. That's the problem when you label all things you don't understand 'evil.'"

"So does that mean you'll be able to free us?" said Cara, shifting around and peering at Molly expectantly.

Molly looked at them all. Her family, and her friends, all tied up. They were counting on her. They needed her.

"I . . . really don't know what I am doing here," she said sheepishly. Molly racked her frazzled brain. Maybe she could use the sparks to . . . set fire to her bindings? No, setting something on fire in a locked room might kill everyone. "Uhh . . ."

"Wait. Molly, if you can hold the machine for a little, *I* can do something," said Marty. "Do you think you can try to lower the energy on the furnace while I untie everyone?"

"Maybe?" said Molly. She closed her eyes and concentrated. Behind her, the Kremragende rumbled.

"I said LOWER!" said Marty.

"Okay, okay!" said Molly, taking a deep breath. Maybe if she just focused on the furnace, focused all of herself on feeling the heat next to her, on imagining it as part of her. Then she willed it to cool, feeling the cold air in front of her flow into the inferno behind her.

"Okay, it's working, Moll!" said Marty. "Keep going!"

A bead of sweat trickled down Molly's brow. "Mm-hmm" was all she could manage to say. She felt Marty untie her and flexed her wrists and hands, eyes still closed. She didn't dare move any farther.

"Dee tied a whole bunch of weird stuff to your wrists, I don't know what," said Marty.

"Hmm, looks like some talismans and amulets . . . oh, and some rue!" said Mr. Bones. "Exactly what I mentioned to you yesterday, Molly, as a way of protecting yourself from the Evil Eye. Isn't that ironic?"

Molly nodded, starting to tremble.

"Is everyone free?" said Dad.

"Yes!" said Grace.

"Marty!" grunted Molly with the last of her energy. "I don't think I can hold this much longer!"

"On it!" he yelled, diving back into the machine. His voice immediately became strained. "That said, I don't know how long *I* can hold it now."

"Okay, everyone, look around. Does anyone see *anything*

at all capable of picking a lock? Or cutting wires?" said Dad, sounding increasingly desperate.

"And something that can either unscrew the front of the furnace, or can pierce through it," added Marty.

Molly was about to translate Marty for Cara and Grace, when she suddenly realized something. . . . "Wait . . . I can do this!" she gasped, still out of breath. "Maybe! At least I snapped the violin string at the concert! And I shattered the glass in multiple lightbulbs!"

Molly turned back to the furnace. "Marty, point at the wire you need me to cut! Literally touch it!"

Deep within the furnace, Molly may not have been able to see or feel the machinery, but she *could* feel Marty straining and pointing. She placed her hands as close to the scalding furnace as she dared. Her eyes started to dry out, her hands shook even more, and her skin felt so hot it seemed like it could melt. She hoped Marty was right. She hoped even more she had enough energy left within her to pierce metal and wire.

There was an icy almost hand on her shoulder. "You can do this, Molly," said her mom. "I know you can."

A warmer hand was on her other shoulder. "You've got this," said her dad, nodding.

A bear hug came from behind now. "And we've got you, Moll," said Timothy.

"Yuuurrhh!" said Dyandra, as Molly felt a small, deceptively strong pair of arms wrap around her knees. She took a deep breath, feeling a little more in control. After all, even if she didn't believe in herself, it was nice to know other people did.

Molly's hands stilled, and she felt a warmth within her. Almost as warm as the furnace, coming from her stomach, and rising, tingling up her chest, down her arms, and through her hands. Then out in front of her now, focused like a sharp spike to where Marty pointed, gaining speed and feeling almost out of Molly's control.

Molly gasped as she was thrown back, as if everything she had pushed into the furnace bounced back to her. Her family caught her (well, mostly Timothy and Dad), and helped her stand up, still winded. The furnace shuddered and heaved before grinding, slowly, to a halt.

Molly looked up to see a small round hole in the side of the furnace, right between where her hands had been. "You did it!" shouted Marty from inside. "Molly, you did it!"

"Molly did it!" yelled Timothy to the others, punching the air.

"Yes!" cheered Cara, hugging Grace. Then everyone hugged, and laughed, and cried, and hugged again. They were going to be okay.

"Hey, Moll! Do you think you can use your powers to get us out of here?" asked Timothy.

"I can give it a go!" said Molly, feeling newly inflated with confidence and energy. She strode over to the door. "I think I've got enough of a handle on this witch thing to do that at least!" She pressed her hands up to the crematorium doors.

There was a massive boom just a few moments later as the doors blew completely off their hinges. They sailed through the evening air and landed on a couple of gravestones a few yards away, knocking one over.

"Hey, Moll," said Timothy with the bright smile of the annoyingly helpful. "I think you should use less power next time."

"Shut up," said Molly.

She squinted across the graveyard. There were a couple of familiar figures watching them from a distance. And after seeing that the Dades were free, the Westons turned and ran.

Chapter
Twenty-Eight

❧

"I'm on it!" yelled Marty. "Poltergeist speed!"

Molly ran after him, her legs shaking. She felt powered by adrenaline and pretty much nothing else. Everyone followed her, racing toward the Westons before they could get away.

Marty was far ahead of them now, catching up to Dee and Ethan, who were almost at Goody Proxmire's hawthorn tree.

They clearly had no idea that there was a Dade gaining on them. Their expressions turned triumphant as they ran toward a plain white van parked nearby.

Marty caught up before they reached it . . . and ran

straight past. He didn't even try to trip or slow them as he passed. What was he thinking? He turned to Molly, grinned, and jumped into Goody Proxmire's tree.

The great branches of the old hawthorn bowed and bent. Long, spindly ones trembled and groaned, reaching out like mummified fingers. They grabbed Ethan and Dee, binding them by the wrists and neck as they screamed.

As Molly ran up, she felt Marty floating inside the trunk. His eyes were closed, almost like he was one with the ancient hawthorn. Maybe Marty might have been a witch, too, Molly thought, had he lived.

The Westons clearly had the same idea, in a round-about way. "This is WITCHCRAFT!" shrieked Ethan into the night, struggling in vain against his twiggy binds. Molly looked around. The streets of Roehampton were mercifully deserted. Everyone was sleeping off Christmas.

Suddenly, Molly felt a whoosh beside her. Mom passed her, her lack of body clearly improving her speed, as she had not been much of a runner in life. She was now pushing back the sleeves of her kaftan, her face a mask of pure fury as she got up close to Dee's face. Molly almost felt frightened for the Westons, or would have had they not just tried to kill her and everyone she loved.

"You horrible, vicious *monsters!*" growled Mom, now in full mama-ghost-bear mode.

"What was that?" said Dee, looking around in terror before turning to Molly. "What have you done, you *witch*?"

"What have *you* done?!" said Mom before Molly could answer. "You *murdered* my little boy! You murdered me! And then you made me think it was my fault!"

Both Dee and Ethan had turned pale. "It's the mom!" gasped Dee.

"But that's impossible," whispered Ethan. "We took all the right precautions! We banished all evil back to hell! How is she still here?"

"Because I'm not evil! And neither is my daughter!" said Mom. "Who you also just tried to kill! Along with my husband and my other children!"

"We were ridding the world of sin and darkness!" said Dee, twisting and turning desperately, but still caught in the tree.

"Sin and darkness?" shrieked Mom. Her kaftan inflated, and she started to float higher, her hair flying about as if underwater. The image was both pretty and scary in a weird way, like watching a cluster of butterflies carry a machete. "You tried to kill five children today!" she screamed. "How's *that* for sin and darkness?" She wound her fist back as if to throw a punch.

Timothy looked skeptical. "Okay, I get that Mom's angry, but what can she do?" he murmured to the rest of them. "She's mostly ectoplasm these days."

Mom's fist was now traveling as if in slow motion toward Dee. Remembering what it looked like when Mom jumped into a *dead* body, Molly suddenly had a suspicion of what her mother was trying to do. She took a deep breath, gathered whatever scrap of energy she could and willed it, forced it out, to make Mom stronger.

Dee's eyes rolled back and she started spasming within her binds. Mom had literally, with Molly's help, punched herself into Dee Weston's body.

"Oh. Oh, that's what Mom can do," said Timothy, looking both scared and impressed.

What looked like Dee blinked her eyes, the same dreamy expression Mom normally had now on her face. "Oh . . . oh, this is strange," she said. "I think she's color-blind! I've never looked at the world like this before. I know it's not the time, but this is actually really inspiring!"

"Well done, honey!" said Dad, looking genuinely proud.

"Uh . . . what should I do?" said Mom-dressed-as-Dee. Ethan was staring at her, frozen to the spot in horror even if he hadn't been trapped by an ancient tree. Behind him, Marty's face lit up.

"I have an idea!" he said. "Molly, do you think you can help me out like you did Mom just then?"

"I can try!" said Molly. "Have you ever possessed anyone before?"

"Who are you talking to?" gasped Ethan, his head swinging around wildly.

"No," said Marty. "But I just saw Mom do it. I think I have the theory down."

"Okay," said Molly, bracing herself. Goody Proxmire's tree released its prisoners as Marty stepped out. Mom-dressed-as-Dee stayed put. Ethan tried to make a run for it.

But Marty was faster. Molly felt her brother leap through the air and swan dive . . . straight into Ethan's ear. This was the first time he'd tried this; she knew she had to help him. Closing her eyes, she willed all the energy she had left toward her brother.

Molly shook, and her legs buckled. It wasn't enough, or at least enough to keep her standing. Helpless, she collapsed to her knees. A pair of vintage jean–clad legs walked toward her.

"Molly?" said Ethan, his voice now warm and friendly. Molly blinked and looked up. Ethan was giving her a very Martyish smirk. "I think it worked. And I have a plan."

Fifteen minutes later, the files had all been uploaded. Molly looked over Ethan's computer screen one last time and hit post. Normally, Marty could be counted on to move everything with his powers, but he was currently occupied. Or more accurately, currently occupying someone.

After checking that everything was showing on the Westons' website, Molly picked up the laptop and stepped out of the Westons' van. It was still parked next to Goody Proxmire's tree, around which her friends and family were preparing for their part in the plan.

"All set!" she called out to them brightly. She was completely ignored.

"And then you press the big red button at the bottom," said Grace to Mom, who was still in Dee's body and ineptly poking at Dee's phone. Mr. Bones observed and shook his head, as did Cara. Dad was trying his best to keep a very bored Dyandra occupied and away from the seagulls.

"No, Mom!" sighed Timothy as he reached over Mom's shoulder to tap the screen. "You still have it on photo! We need to post a *video!*"

"I had it on video!" said Mom indignantly.

"You really didn't," said Marty-Ethan.

"Do you need me to hel— AARGH!" said Cara as she was tackled by Dyandra.

"I am *so* sorry, Cara," said Dad as he pulled Dyandra off her. "Dyandra! Charging people is *not okay!* We've talked about this, young la—"

"GUYS!" yelled Molly. Everyone turned and looked.

Rather than shrinking at the attention like she would normally, Molly took a deep breath and stood up straighter. After nearly dying, wrangling her loved ones now seemed much less stressful in comparison. "Hey. The files are uploaded, so we should do this now!"

"Okay!" said Timothy. He took the phone from Mom and pressed the appropriate buttons, before taking a step back. "*I'll* record, Mom. Ready when you guys are!"

Marty-as-Ethan and Mom-as-Dee gathered. "Ready!" said Marty. "And Molly's right, we should hurry. Ethan wants to get me ou— WITCH, YOU WILL PAY!" Ethan's features momentarily returned to his previous expression of fury, before snapping back into something more pleasant. "Sorry, Moll, I am trying to get a handle on him, but I've never done this before."

"Okay, you good now, Marty?" said Timothy. Marty-dressed-as-Ethan nodded. "Annnd, you're on!" Mom and Marty, or Ethan and Dee, immediately turned their attention back to the camera.

"This is Dee from *Myth and Wessons*," said Mom.

"*Myth and* Westons," said Marty. "And I'm Ethan."

"Yes! And we want to make a confession," said Mom, glancing over at Molly. She smiled. "We are *very bad people.*"

"That's right!" said Marty. "In fact, we are *serial killers!*"

"I know, we look like completely normal, fashionably

dressed podcasters," said Mom. "It was all a cover! For our vicious cross-country killing spree! We are responsible for the deaths of several innocent people!"

"This is not a joke!" said Marty. "We have uploaded evidence of several murders to the link in the caption. You can view everything there! We are terrible, terrible human beings! And we are telling you this because . . . uh . . . because . . ."

"Because we are so bad we are proud of it!" said Mom. "We killed Marty and Julia Dade last year! And we just tried to kill the rest of the Dades and three of their friends just now! But they escaped! And, uh . . . we want them to know that we will be back!"

"Yeah!" said Marty. "Because, to reiterate, we are literal serial killers! Once again, you can see all the evidence for our crimes at the link below. Stay spooky!"

"Why did you say that?" said Mom, looking confused. "Stay spooky?"

"It's how they—*we* end every podcast," said Marty, smiling desperately to the camera.

"Oh!" said Mom. "Okay! Stay spooky and have a good day, everyone!"

"And done!" said Timothy. He tapped at Dee's phone for a few moments. "I've just posted it to all of their social media channels." He chuckled as he checked the phone again. "Oh man, the comments already!"

"And I called 911," said Cara. "They should be here soon."

Marty and Mom, still in borrowed bodies, collapsed to the ground. Molly watched as they floated out, leaving the Westons' unconscious bodies behind. Ethan and Dee didn't seem to be going anywhere in a hurry.

"Is it . . . is it over?" said Molly. Sirens rang out in the distance.

"I think so," said Mom. "Are you okay, sweetie? You must have used up a lot of energy doing everything you did today."

"You saved us, Molly!" said Dad. "You and Marty!"

"Well, Cara warned us first," said Molly, looking over at Cara, who smiled back.

"And you can blow doors off stuff!" said Timothy. "Which is just wicked cool!"

"We're all just so proud of you," said Mom.

"We really are," said Dad.

"Hyuuuuuurgh!" said Dyandra.

"Oh, guys," said Molly, wiping away a tear. Everyone gathered around her for a group hug. Even Mr. Bones, though Dyandra impeded him a little by trying to climb his left leg.

"Dy-Dy . . ." said Mom and Dad reproachfully when they noticed, but Mr. Bones cut them off.

"It's quite all right," he said. "I think after today, we could all do with letting off a little steam." Dyandra had reached his shoulders now and launched herself off them. Mr. Bones almost maintained balance and was saved by Dad.

Meanwhile, Timothy caught Dyandra expertly. "Oh, looks like I have a Dy-Dy ball!" he said as he swung her back and forth. Dyandra squealed with delight.

Molly looked at the loving chaos that was her friends and family, and smiled. She felt her shoulders unclench. It really was over.

She was starting to feel almost relaxed again when she heard an engine starting behind her.

As everyone realized what was happening, the Westons' white van drove straight past them and sped down the winding narrow streets of Roehampton. It took a sharp left and drove out of sight, tires screeching. Molly looked over to the tree. Ethan and Dee were no longer in the crumpled pile that they'd left them in.

"They're getting away!" yelled out Timothy. "We need to stop them!"

"We can't," said Dad. "Just be glad we're all still here. In spirit in some cases, but still here."

Molly held up the Westons' laptop. "And between this and the phone, we have plenty of evidence against them."

"You saved it? Yes, Molly!" said Grace. "Ethan and Dee will be less likely to come back to Roehampton if they're wanted criminals . . . right?"

Molly looked down the street where Dee and Ethan had made their escape. Grace had a point. It *would* be risky for them to return.

All the same, Molly could still remember the expressions on the Westons' faces as they looked at her family, even now. Pure hatred. The kind of pure hatred that made people reckless enough to stage two explosions in the span of a year at the same location.

Molly shuddered and turned to Grace uneasily. "Right…" she said, more out of hope than agreement. "Right."

Chapter
Twenty-Nine

Several hours later, everyone had given their statements to the police. The Dades handed over the Westons' laptop and phone, and the crematorium was roped off as a crime scene. Grace's and Cara's parents had come, hugged their children while sobbing loudly, and then taken them home. Molly and her family were just finishing up at the police station when Mr. Bones rushed over.

"Oh, I'm so glad I caught you!" he gasped. "It's just that whilst I was sitting anticipating my impending demise in the crematorium back there, a few things occurred to me. I meant to bring it up with you all earlier but I was distracted, what with all the excitement and possessing that followed. It concerns Dyandra."

"Hurgh?" said Dyandra, looking up with interest as she climbed up Timothy's leg.

"Yes. You see, I've actually theorized for some time that Dyandra might not be infectious," said Mr. Bones. "Once I saw with my own eyes that zombies were real, I got interested and read up on the topic."

"Okay . . ." said Molly.

Mr. Bones continued. "As far as I can tell, there haven't been any recorded cases of zombieism spreading through bites in real life. It may even have been made up by Hollywood."

"You don't say," said Dad.

"I do! In fact, the only credible instances that I have found, which is honestly difficult the way the internet is these days, all seem to be done by witches," said Mr. Bones. "So when Molly and Marty thought they were cursed by a witch, I kept my mind open. But I was stumped with regard to what the witch's motive could be. Why resurrect Dyandra and leave her to be cared for by the very people she cursed?"

"Hurrghh . . ." said Dyandra thoughtfully as she swung from Timothy's neck. He was beginning to turn purple but continued smiling good-naturedly.

"And then when we found out today that Molly was the witch all along . . ." said Mr. Bones, "well, it all fits, doesn't it? I suspect Molly's grief was so powerful that it reanimated the nearest whole dead body."

"I see," said Dad.

"So what you're saying is, because Dyandra was turned into a zombie by Molly, she probably isn't dangerous to the living?" said Mom. "That's wonderful."

"Exactly!" said Mr. Bones. "People shouldn't be affected by Dyandra's bites. As long as they are all up-to-date with their jabs, they should be fine."

"Still, do we want to risk it?" said Molly.

"I'm happy to test it out myself. Come on, Dyandra, let's have that mouth guard of yours," said Mr. Bones, rolling up a sleeve. "Have at it."

Before Molly could stop either of them, Dyandra leaped off Timothy and ran over to Mr. Bones, her neon-pink mouth guard clattering to the ground. She opened her mouth, still mostly filled with small, sharp teeth, and bit into Mr. Bones's outstretched arm.

"AAAARGH!" screamed the Dades collectively.

Over the next few days, Molly and her family watched Mr. Bones from a distance, just in case he started grunting or trying to eat their heads. They could handle a three-year-old zombie, but a fully grown adult seemed like more of a challenge. Instead, Mr. Bones merely put antiseptic and a Band-Aid on the bite mark and went about his life as usual.

After a week passed, and Mr. Bones didn't get any more undead-seeming than he normally did, the Dades finally breathed easy. As a result, Dyandra now got to go without a mouth guard around the house at least. They still kept it on in public in case she tried to eat the replacement ducks in Roehampton Pond, and even that was a work in progress. The Dades were experimenting with various animal brains from the butcher, and they seemed to be doing a lot for her formerly insatiable cravings.

Dyandra was sitting mouth guard–free right now on Dad's lap. His sweaters had started developing a lot more holes of late, but he didn't seem to mind. It was a lazy Sunday afternoon, and everyone had gathered around the Dades' large fireplace. Grace had also joined them, to both toast marshmallows and discuss whether to tell Dave and Ben the truth about the Dades.

"We all think you should feel free to tell your dads about what's going on with us," Mom was saying to her. "In your own time of course. But we just want you to know we've discussed it, and we think we can trust both of them with our big secret. It's really up to you."

"I know Cara's telling her parents, or maybe she has

already," added Molly. "We figured since her mom's a selkie, too, they'd be cool with it. And obviously they know how to keep secrets, so we told her to go ahead."

"I do want to tell my dads soon," said Grace, nodding. "But not *yet*. After everything that happened with the Westons last week, I think they need some time to deal with me nearly getting murdered before I spring ghosts, zombies, and witches on them. I just want to ease them in, you know?"

"Completely understandable," said Dad as Dyandra unraveled his sweater with her teeth.

"Hey, we're on the news again!" said Timothy, his head buried in his phone. "Kaitlyn just texted me. 'The FBI is set to reopen the Julia and Martin Dade case, following shocking events last week.'"

"Any more sightings of Dee and Ethan?" said Marty.

"One alleged sighting in a gas station in New Mexico, but other than that, no," said Timothy. He brightened. "Maybe they *did* get scared off for good."

"I hope s—" said Molly, but she was cut off by the clanging chimes of their doorbell.

Molly ran to answer, finding Cara on the doorstep. "I brought my mom," she said, pointing to the preppily dressed woman standing next to her. Molly recognized her from the police station last week.

"Hi, Molly," said Cara's mom. "Cara's already filled me

in on everything going on with your family. I actually wanted to talk to your mom about something related."

"Sure? Right this way," said Molly, leading them to the living room, completely confused as to what a selkie would want with a ghost. "Mom, Cara's mom—"

"Fiona," said Cara's mom. "Great to properly meet you. Especially under better circumstances than at the station!"

"Julia, and definitely!" said Mom.

"So Cara tells me you know all about our big family secret," said Fiona, smiling. "And she also let me in on yours. I hope that's okay."

"Of course! And I have to say, it's nice to speak with another supernatural Roehampton parent. I thought I was the only one!" said Mom.

"Me too!" said Fiona. "It's such a *big* relief to be able to talk to someone about this stuff other than my family. You try to explain to someone that you are an aquatic mammal part-time!"

"Oh, I bet!" said Mom. "Would you like a drink? I can't pick anything up, but I can point the way."

"Sounds great!" said Fiona as she followed Mom in the direction of the kitchen.

"What's this all about?" said Molly to Cara.

"Ghost book club," said Cara. "Mom spotted some ghosts heading into the lighthouse when she was in seal form a while back. She asked them what was going on, and apparently they hold a book club there every two weeks. That's why the light keeps turning on. It's much easier for the ghosts to read that way."

"Ohhhh," said Molly.

"So my dad was right!" said Grace. "That lighthouse *does* get turned on by ghosts. Much less scary ghosts than we were expecting, but still!"

"Yep," said Cara. "Anyway, my mom thought your mom would be interested."

There was a burst of middle-aged female laughter from the kitchen. "They seem to be hitting it off," said Molly. "And I know Mom will be glad to make some new friends. She's been pretty lonely since the accident."

"And I'm pleased that the rest of the Dade women are making new friends, too," said Dad. "We still can't thank you enough, Cara, for all that you've done for us. We literally owe you our lives."

"It's no problem." Cara shrugged.

"No, I mean it," said Dad, looking very pleased with what he was about to say. "You certainly have our *seal of approval.*"

As Cara smiled politely, Molly groaned. "Dad, don't."

Incredibly, Cara did not leave immediately after hearing Dad's joke. Instead, she stuck around and hung out with Molly, Marty, and Grace, and even let Dyandra climb on her. Meanwhile, Mom and Fiona talked for several hours. In the end, everyone stayed so long that the Dades decided to order pizza, and Grace, Cara, and her mom stayed for dinner.

And it was a nice meal. Even though they had to translate for Marty now and two family members no longer ate, it was practically like old times. Molly had almost forgotten what it was like having people over—they used to do it all the time before the accident.

So all in all, she should have been feeling better. They had saved the day after all. And beaten the bad guys. Even what she'd thought was a curse turned out to be magic powers. Instead, Molly felt strangely hollow all dinner, even as she smiled along with everyone's jokes.

It only got worse after everyone left. Molly slumped to her room, the hollow feeling intensifying to something that nearly felt like sadness. Exhausted, she fell on her bed and absentmindedly began stroking the dead cat still under there.

"Can I come in?" said a ghostly voice at the door.

Molly sat halfway up. "Sure," she said, feeling very unsure.

Her mom floated through the door, and sat next to her on

the bed. "How are you feeling?" she asked, placing a spectral hand on Molly's shoulder, or as much as she could manage.

"I'm okay," said Molly. Mom did not look like she believed her.

"Is that a 'you are *really* okay'?" said Mom. "Or more a 'you would *like* to be okay'?"

Molly sighed and sat up all the way. "I would like to be, I guess. I mean I *should* be. You're still here, Marty's still here, and we have Dyandra now. We are safe . . . probably. What do I have to feel sad about?"

"Well, even if you aren't grieving *us*, you can still grieve the life we had before the accident," said Mom. "I know I do. There were so many things I loved doing that I can't do anymore. So many plans I had that are now impossible without a body. A lot has changed, even if we are all still together."

Molly didn't say anything because she was afraid she would sob, so she just nodded. A fat tear rolled down her cheek, betraying her anyway.

"Oh, honey, it's okay," said Mom. "So much has changed, and so fast. It would be weird if you didn't feel sad about it. There's nothing wrong with not liking that at all." Molly was crying openly now, and she felt the icy air around her as her mom hugged her. It was oddly comforting, if freezing.

"B-but we might be okay *now*," sobbed Molly, "but what happens in the future? Will Marty age? Or will he be a kid forever, and then I'll be *old* . . ." Her voice cracked as she was unable to finish the sentence.

"I don't know," said Mom. "And yes, that's hard when you don't know. It's one of those things that we can only take as it comes, and deal with it then. But you know what? We can face it all together. After everything we've been through, I think we get to call ourselves real survivors." She looked down at her ghostly body. "In a manner of speaking."

Molly rubbed her face. "It's not just Marty. What about you? A-and then Dyandra, what will happen to her?"

"Well, imagine that we don't age," said Mom. "If that's the case, maybe we can become the family guardians. We'll watch over you and Timothy, and any kids you might have, and your kids' kids. Just like Mr. Bones's family ghost. I don't think that sounds too bad."

Molly smiled and nodded shakily. "Though maybe you guys could be a little less . . . pushy than Old Mother Bones. Seeing as Mr. Bones moved here to get away from her."

"Nngh," said Dyandra through the door, clearly disagreeing. Normally, Molly was annoyed by Dyandra's eavesdropping, but this time she caught her mom's eye. They both burst into a fit of giggles.

"And if none of this had happened, we wouldn't have Dyandra, would we?" said Mom as Dyandra barreled into the room and sat on Molly's lap. Molly gave her a hug.

The little zombie was being especially cute and she knew it.

"I guess what I'm saying is, just because things don't turn out the way we wanted or the way we planned doesn't mean that we can't be happy," said Mom. "And even if we do feel sad right now, it doesn't mean we will feel that way forever. Does that make sense?"

Molly nodded. She was beginning to feel better. Maybe she would be okay after all. Or if not okay, perhaps she might be able to handle it.

Dyandra threw her arms around her neck and hugged her. Molly smiled at her mom. In fact, all her family might. They had one another.

Epilogue

The next semester started with even more whispers than usual. Now that the Dades had made national news, there was really no escaping it. But something else had changed. Normally, Molly would have been self-conscious and stressed out. Now she found herself strangely not caring.

After all, she had Grace back as her true best friend, with no secrets between them. And Marty was still her partner in crime. And most incredibly of all, Cara Hartman, her former mortal enemy, now had her back and was busy sending death glares to anyone who dared try to hint anything negative about Molly. As Cara ruled her friendship group with an iron grip that most dictators would be envious of, this did much to quell a lot of the rumors.

Molly was sitting next to Cara right now, Marty on the other side. With Ms. Lewis's blessing, he was assisting them in their Roehampton witch trial project, which was going much more smoothly now that Molly and Cara had buried the hatchet.

"I actually found something out related to you guys this weekend," said Cara, pulling some printed paper out of her bag. "I got to look in the archives at Brodie College—Daddy knows the dean. Anyway, I was looking over anything they had on the witch trials, and I found the original court transcripts. . . ."

"I'm sorry, Molly, can I have a quick word?" said Ms. Lewis. Molly looked up, and felt her stomach drop instinctively. Even though Ms. Lewis was clued in to their situation now, Molly was so used to evading her personal questions that old habits died hard.

"Sure, Ms. Lewis," said Molly, scrambling to her feet. She didn't like the serious expression on Ms. Lewis's face either, like they were about to have a difficult talk.

"So," began Ms. Lewis once they had reached a suitably secluded corner of the library, "I wanted to speak to you about the recent . . . events."

Molly nodded and shifted awkwardly on her feet. She flexed her fingers. The last thing she needed was her magic going off now.

"And also, more importantly," said Ms. Lewis, "the fact that you seem to be displaying witch powers."

Molly's jaw dropped, but she was too stunned for a response. Ms. Lewis filled in the silence for her.

"I'm a descendant of Goody Proxmire, remember?" explained Ms. Lewis. "I've been a witch since before I even started teaching."

"But when did you find out about me?" said Molly, still trying to process everything Ms. Lewis was saying. "And how did you know?"

"I've suspected ever since that basketball game last year. Making animals fall from the sky is a classic sign of witch powers manifesting. One of my own coven realized he was a witch when he accidentally made koi carp rain on his dad and stepmom on their wedding day," said Ms. Lewis. "Then after the accident, I could see that you were still talking to Marty, and that helped narrow down who the witch was. The Christmas concert really sealed it."

"Wait, you knew Marty was here the *whole time?!*" said Molly.

"Well, sensing ghosts for witches is more like . . . tuning in to the right radio frequency. I can't hear him unless I concentrate," said Ms. Lewis. "Which I only did once I suspected you were talking to him. I'm pretty sure I heard you say 'Shut up, Marty' at one point."

"Oh . . ." said Molly.

"Though the fact that you and your family can all just hear him, and that *everyone* can hear your mom is pretty unusual," said Ms. Lewis. "And Marty's way with electronics. Your family really aren't normal ghosts."

"My family really aren't normal anything," said Molly.

Ms. Lewis laughed. "I meant that in a good way. I'd love to look into it some more. It's rare to have ghosts so present with the living—I really haven't come across anything like it. It's why I acted so shocked when your family told me officially about your situation."

"Oh, I thought maybe you were just good at acting," said Molly.

"Well, I have had a few roles in local theater productions." Ms. Lewis preened. "But in this case I was genuinely surprised. I knew that Marty was still here at that point, but the fact that your mom stuck around too was news to me. And the fact that I could hear her without trying . . . I could barely believe it. I wonder if that has something to do with your witch powers as well."

"We have a theory I brought them back, and Dyandra, too, because I was so stressed out when they died," said Molly.

"Yes, that makes sense," said Ms. Lewis. "Times of stress and high emotion tend to cause some major powers to leak out. I wanted to offer to help you out and show you how to handle them—"

"Oh, that's why you kept asking if I had anything to tell you," said Molly as Ms. Lewis nodded.

"I know from experience that having your abilities come out is a lot, especially without any guidance. I just didn't know if you were ready to talk about it yet."

"I actually didn't know it was me doing all those things until recently," said Molly. "I was just really confused."

"Oof, I bet," said Ms. Lewis. "And now I realize that you were targeted by witch hunters . . . Molly, I'm just so sorry I didn't reach out sooner."

"Oh, it's okay!" said Molly. "I don't think it would have made sense to me if you had. I actually thought everything that was happening was because I had been cursed by Goody Proxmire, not that I had my *own* witch powers."

"Oh, Goody Proxmire didn't curse anyone. That's just a legend," said Ms. Lewis. "The story passed down in my family is that she did the *exact opposite.*"

"What do you mean?" said Molly.

"Well, Goody Proxmire knew that she was coming to the end of her life anyway. Witches often do. So she decided to peace out with a bang," said Ms. Lewis. "She said her good-byes to her children and grandchildren, and cast a final spell. The most powerful one of her life. One she put all her magic and energy into, knowing she wasn't going to use them where she was going."

"What kind of a spell?" said Molly.

"A powerful binding spell," said Ms. Lewis. "That made Roehampton a place of safety for magical folks . . . like witches, for example. And after that point, the Roehampton witch trials fizzled out. No further people were executed, unlike at Salem."

"Because of her spell!" said Molly.

"Right," said Ms. Lewis. "You see, Goody Proxmire was head of the coven of good witches that your ancestor was part of. Cunning folk, they were called in those days. Goody Proxmire wanted to make sure they were safe, even when she was gone."

"So all the weird stuff in Roehampton isn't because she cursed the town?" said Molly.

"No," said Ms. Lewis. "It's because she *protected* the town for us magical types. A spell so powerful that it's still holding strong to this day. As a result, Roehampton seems to attract people of a supernatural nature, sometimes when they aren't even aware of it. Your family is a perfect example."

"And Mr. Bones," said Molly in wonder. "And Car—" She managed to stop herself almost in time and felt immediately guilty. Ms. Lewis however smiled knowingly.

"Ah, yes," she said. "Like I told your parents the other

day, when you've been teaching in Roehampton as long as I have, you see families come in *all* shapes and sizes. I miiight have deliberately put you in a group with someone hoping you would realize quite how much you have in common. And I'm glad to see that you have finally ended the rivalry."

Molly looked over at Cara, who was texting intensely on her phone, and Marty, who was sending messages back. If someone had told her this would be happening even a few weeks ago, she never would have believed it.

"One last thing, and I'll let you get back to them," said Ms. Lewis. "Would you like some after-school lessons in witchcraft? I'll reach out to your parents, too, but I wanted to bring it up with you first. If you're just starting out, there will be much less risk of accidents if you have someone around to show you the ropes. I say this as someone who once accidentally blew up my parents' back deck when I was your age."

"That would be great!" said Molly. "Thanks, Ms. Lewis!"

"Don't mention it!" said Ms. Lewis, before adding in a much quieter voice. "But really, don't mention it. It's easier for us witches if we're kept quiet, too."

Molly nodded and walked back stunned to where Cara and Marty were sitting. "Marty," she said as she sat down, "I don't think a witch cursed our house after all!"

"But—" said Marty.

"No, I'm serious! Goody Proxmire actually cast a spell to

protect magical folk like us! Ms. Lewis told me, I'll explain later when we're not at school," said Molly. "So I guess all the times that our house has been burned down or hit by hurricanes or lightning was, I dunno, bad luck or something. Weird, huh?"

"Yeah . . . about that . . ." said Marty.

Cara's phone beeped. "Okay, Marty says you should see these," she said, handing over one of the printouts she had brought to Molly. "They're the transcripts from the witch trials themselves. Specifically, the part where Solomon Hapgood, aka the original cemetery keeper, gave his testimony."

Molly looked at the paper. It was a scan of an extremely old and weathered page, the text wobbly and hard to read due to the handwriting and spelling.

> Thenne Solomon Hapgood didst swear upon An Oath that Goody Proxmire was indeed in league with the Great Serpent, and beat upon his breast in great agitation. He proclaimed further that if he didst tell a lye, thenne he, his descendants, and the lande upon which he worked shall thenceforth be forever Cursed.

> Upon sayinge this, he didst collapse in the stande, and was taken forthwith to his house whereupon he hath yet to recover. The court was shocked by this most wicked and obvious act of witchery, and it hath been entered into Goody Proxmire's record of unholy acts upon which she is to be further tried.

"So . . . what are you saying?" said Molly when she had finished reading.

"That even if a *witch* didn't curse our house, and the cemetery," said Marty, "it looks like maybe a witch *hunter* did by accident. By telling a lie under oath."

"I don't know . . ." said Molly. "I mean is this really proof that our house is cursed?"

"He collapsed in the stand right away!" said Marty. "And our home keeps on getting burned down or exploded! I don't think that's bad luck, I think that this guy accidentally caused the curse."

"But Roehampton is supposed to be protected!" said Molly.

"You said for magical folk, not for everyone. And if the blessing is real, who's to say this curse isn't real, too? Maybe the reason we even attracted Ethan and Dee in the first place is because we live on cursed land! After all, you are a magical person, and so's Dyandra and Mr. Bones. Shouldn't you all be protected? And look what happened!" said Marty as Cara's phone buzzed furiously.

"You have a point. I didn't want you to, but you do," said Molly, rubbing her eyes. "Okay, the curse might not be Goody Proxmire's, but it looks like it is real. Ugh, I just want this to be over!"

"Me too," said Marty. "Though on the bright side I guess

that does officially prove that Goody Proxmire was not in league with the Great Serpent. That's something, right?"

"True. That is something." Molly nodded. She paused for a moment. "Though I don't think we can include that part in our witch trial presentation."

After school ended, Molly and Marty headed straight to their probably (still) cursed home. They wanted to tell everyone as soon as possible, and after everything that had happened last year, their parents swore to listen to them if anything like this came up again. They most likely did not expect it to be so soon.

Storm clouds gathered ominously overhead. "Molly . . ." said Marty as low thunder rolled, and the wind picked up.

"That's not me this time!" said Molly, flexing her hands to avoid any pins and needles. "At least, I don't think it is. . . ."

They went in through the back door, straight into the kitchen. Their family was already gathered there, Timothy with his head in his phone, and Mom and Dad trying to get Dyandra down from the top of the cabinet.

"Hey, everyone!" said Molly brightly as she entered the room. "We have something we need to tell y—"

"Dyandra! You need to get down now!" said Mom. "This is not a game."

"Timothy, could you get the mirror?" said Dad as Dyandra expertly dodged his outstretched hands.

"Wha?" said Timothy, turning from his phone briefly, looking slightly dazed. "What do I need to get?"

"GUYS!" yelled Molly.

Everyone turned and stared at her. Even Dyandra.

Molly smiled, and stood up straighter. "So, guys, we have something really important we need to tell you. It's to do with the curse on our house, and—" She was cut off by the brightest flash of lightning she had ever seen, followed by thunder so loud it made the room shake. Then their smoke alarm started going off.

The Dades rushed out of their increasingly hazy kitchen and into the safety of the cemetery. After calling 911, they stood and watched flames engulf what used to be the ground floor bathroom extension, now split open like a piñata. A column of smoke poured into the dusty mauve twilight, sparks spitting and flickering like new stars. Then it started snowing on them.

Molly looked at Marty, who looked at her, sighed, and turned to the rest of their family.

"So yeah," he said. "We *really* need to do something about that curse."

Acknowledgments

Many thanks to agent extraordinaire Pam Gruber for getting me in touch with the lovely folks at MDLC Studios and also for managing to handle me. Seriously, thank you.

Many thanks as well to Melissa de la Cruz for coming up with Molly and her family in the first place, to Britt Rubiano for her expert guidance and edits, and to both for their appreciation for mystery, myths, and dad jokes, as well as for being excellent to work with.

Yet more thanks to Larissa Zageris, my oftentimes partner in writing, and perhaps one day crime if we ever manage to pull off that bank heist. And a final thanks to my most splendid husband Tristan Cooper, for his encouragement, support, and cuddles. Having you two in my corner really helped me get this book over the finish line.